My Invisible Boyfriend

Also by Susie Day:

serafina67 *urgently requires life*

My Invisible
Boyfriend

Susie Day

 SCHOLASTIC PRESS/NEW YORK

Library of Congress Cataloging-in-Publication Data

Day, Susie (Susanna Mary), 1975–
My invisible boyfriend / by Susie Day.
p. cm.
Summary: In a British alternative high school, fifteen-year-old Heidi stands out in many ways, but when she invents a boyfriend — complete with online profile — her friends turn to him for advice and she must decide how far she is willing to go to find acceptance.
ISBN: 978-0-545-07354-7
[1. Interpersonal relations — Fiction. 2. Dating (Social customs) — Fiction. 3. Boarding schools — Fiction. 4. Schools — Fiction. 5. Theater — Fiction. 6. Email — Fiction. 7. England — Fiction.] I. Title.
PZ7.D3327My 2010
[Fic] — dc22
2009004377

10 9 8 7 6 5 4 3 2 1   10 11 12 13 14
Book design by Becky Terhune
First edition, April 2010

Printed in the U. S. A.   23

○ ○

FOR TINA, ABSURDLY BRILLIANT SISTER
AND LOCATOR OF THE CARROT CAKE
— SD

○ ○

My Invisible Boyfriend

Recipe for a Heidi

INGREDIENTS:

Hair (braided)
Two eyes (brown)
Assorted other body parts
Epic collection of *Mycroft Christie Investigates* DVDs
Detective skills
Tendency to fall in love with imaginary people

METHOD:

• Whisk all ingredients with parental implements until thoroughly mixed up.
• Dump resulting goop (including parental implements) in the Goldfinch School for Troublemaking Dropout Freaks.
• Remove Troublemaking Dropout Freaks for summer holidays.
• Bake until mental.

You know your life is not exactly normal when you're sitting on the steps on the first day of school, sugar-high giddy from knowing they're about to unlock the doors.

But then no one at the Finch is normal. They only send you here when you've been kicked out of every other boarding school on the planet — if your parents can afford it. Unless you're me, when it's the Mothership and Dad Man who can't seem to stay still. I've usually just about figured out where the girls' toilets are by the time the Mothership decides that, 300 miles away, there are *other* girls with wobbly thighs who absolutely need her to be the one making them run round and round a hockey pitch in the rain. And then we're off. Dad Man gets a new old van full of paint pots to drive around some new old school buildings. I get a new old bedroom, in the bit of an ex-chemistry lab that's now Staff Housing. Everything else stays the same.

At least it did until we ended up here at the Finch. I mean, I started out like always: the period I like to think of as the Never-ending Era of Pathetic Noobishness, where I eat lunch on my own, and sit in class on my own, and discover that someone has stapled a dissected frog to my backpack so I'm going to be known as Frog Girl till we leave on my own. And then one day, I was sitting on the end of the balance beam that pokes out of the PE stores by the garages, waiting for the Mothership to drive us back down Heart Attack Hill (no Staff Housing for us this time, not when there are so many "dubious influences" around), and Fili came to say hello. Not that she actually said hello, obviously. Fili doesn't do that sort of conversation. She just perched on the beam, and swung her boots, and lent me one earbud so we could listen to some noise. Same thing the next day. We sat together in French, because she's really good at French. And then I met Ludo and Big Dai, and Heidi the Frog Girl was gone forever.

It's funny how you don't know how much you want something till you get it, sometimes. It's like Mycroft Christie says in episode 1.7, "The Pinocchio Man": *Deep down, Jori, we all simply want to* belong.

Mycroft Christie, in case you live under some kind of rock, is the most brilliant person in the universe, and totally my boyfriend. Sort of. Technically, he's not real. Technically, he's the debonair twenty-third-century time-traveling hero of the best! TV show! ever! *Mycroft Christie Investigates* is not actually going to turn up on my doorstep anytime soon to whisk me away to fangirl heaven. Mostly because he's time-trapped in present-day London pretending to be a detective for complicated plot reasons. And because he's obviously in crazypants love with his foxy arse-kicking side-kick Jori Song (with whom he fights crime and has Unresolved Sexual Tension). And also because they canceled the show after three seasons, so now he only really exists inside my DVD player. But he's dashing, and charming, and conveniently available at the flick of a remote control, which is the sort of thing a girl finds handy when she's stuck with the Mothership and Dad Man's board-game obsession for company all summer.

Downside of not being Frog Girl: Once you have some, you really miss your friends when they aren't around.

The holidays haven't been a total disaster. I mean, sure, everyone else has been off to exotic locations courtesy of Guilty Parent Airlines, while I've been slinging scones at tourists in the Little Leaf café. Fili's been visiting the ancient grandmother in Senegal, Ludo's been on Daddy's yacht, and Big Dai went on safari with his sister's family. Me, I got to wear sunglasses once all summer, and that was only because I lost a bet with Betsy and she made me dress up as Nighttime Roller Disco Harry Potter for a whole afternoon. (Betsy is my boss. She's not very sensible. The scones are yummy, though. As is her son, Teddy, who makes them. Sometimes he "accidentally" makes a whole extra batch at the end of the day, so I have to take some home — though that mostly happens when The Lovely Safak is around. That's his very tall, very beautiful girlfriend, who is also very nice so I can't even hate her. Sigh.)

But none of that matters now. Finchworld is starting again. Sneaking up to the dorm rooms (where Nonresident Students, i.e., me, aren't supposed to be allowed), to lie on Fili's bed, IMing gossip from one side of the room to the other (in a very intellectual, non–Scheherezade Adams-y kind of way). Watching *Mycroft Christie Investigates* for the bajillionth time, with me and Dai doing our special carpet-slapping dance to the theme song. Searching for kittens on YouTube and eating toast. And, you know, math tests and stuff. But I don't care about those bits. I can ignore those bits. The rest is going to be spectacular.

SPECK.

TACK.

YOU.

LA.

(You're allowed "LA" in Scrabble. According to Dad Man anyway. I think he might be a CHEATER — seven-letter word, fifty extra points.)

I hear a scrape behind me, and Dad Man's face appears, scrunching as he drags back the huge oak doors of the Manor house. I look down the long driveway as the first of a line of Mercedes eases through the gates at the bottom of the hill.

"You coming in, then, love?" says Dad Man, yawning because he's been up here since this morning, dragging luggage about. "There's a few been here since lunchtime, had early flights."

I'm already skipping up the wide stone steps of the posh for-the-parents entrance with its funny square hedges on spikes, because the details of those with early flights may just possibly have been written on my calendar, and in my phone, and on the back of my hand in red felt pen, just in case.

"Try the common room," he shouts after me as I skid along the polished floor of the hall, past the notice boards and empty offices.

And there she is, sitting on the squishy blue sofa in front of the plasma screen, eating an orange. Filicia Mathilde Diouf, the world's blackest Goth, all silver rings and eyeliner and that one sarky raised eyebrow that says "hi" and "I missed you, too," and "now stop standing in the doorway like a dork" all on its own.

I grin and flop down on the sofa beside her.

She offers me a piece of orange, then looks me up and down. "Nice coat."

"Detective," I explain.

The Coat is my Thing right now. It's a raincoat: one of those belted beige ones that old pervs wear in parks to flash people. I found it in a cardboard box in the Finch garages, after an afternoon's dust'n'spider battling with Dad Man. I've decided it was left there by some ancient teacher, who figured out the only way to escape the Goldfinch was to flee secretly in the nighttime, leaving all his possessions behind. Old Stinky Mancoat sounds disgusting, I know, but I kind of like the way it skims the ground. It flaps out behind me when I'm on the Bike o' Doom, in a not uncapelike, vaguely super-heroic manner. It makes me feel very detect-y. I kind of love it.

The fact that Mycroft Christie also wears one is totally a coincidence.

Fili nods. Eats more orange. Flicks pips away with a flash of silver rings.

With anyone else, the silence would be awkward. With Fili, it's just proof that she likes you. And anyway, there's a shriek from outside, echoing off the walls of the corridor, announcing the arrival of our resident noisemaker.

"HEIDIIII!"

A human cannonball with invisible jet-pack attachment flies through the door and flings its skinny arms around me. Also hair. Lots of hair, all glossy and dark and a bit more in my mouth than is pleasant. I miss a few sentences while trying to escape. These little details do not worry Ludo.

"... and the traffic was, like, AWFUL and I was totally UNPLEASED, because I wasn't even going to GET here, and there's, like, THE party tonight, and I have SO much to tell you before we even get to that, only you will SO not believe OH MY GOD, FILI! You're here! I didn't even KNOW you were here!"

Fili receives the hair-in-face treatment, too. Ludo keeps talking. Fili rolls her eyes, and shoves a wet chunk of orange in Ludo's mouth. It slows her down to a mumble for all of five seconds.

"OH MY GOD, I've missed you SO much!"

She hugs us together again, and I find myself grinning like a loony. This is what I've been waiting for, for months. All we need now is Big Dai and we'll be set: Team Finch, Finch Force Four, the Leftover Squad, reunited for another term of thrilling adventures. The credits are about to roll, introducing Ludo, sexy-beautiful wild child; Fili, enigmatic tech witch; Dai, the big guy with the heart of gold; and me, Heidi, the fledgling detective whose geekiness is actually strangely attractive. Together we'll fight crime and/or homework, guided by our mentor, Betsy, who'll supply us with our undercover missions via coded messages hidden in cupcakes. We'll have our own theme tune. And costumes. We'll be magnificent.

They don't actually know any of this yet, obviously. That's how undercover we are.

A couple of hours later, once I can't see the TV for bodies, I realize I'm at the McCartney Party.

At the start of each term, there's a blowout. The Upper School kids have to use up all the contraband hidden in their suitcases before it gets confiscated, but the real prize is to get kicked out before school even begins — all in loving memory of STUART A. MCCARTNEY, 1979. McCartney is a legend. No one knows exactly what he did to get the boot. The story probably changes every year. But his name's on the Student of the Year board, carved into wood, painted gold, and hung in the entrance hall where he stays, inspiration to all. The McCartney Party's not exactly invite-only: You just need to know where it is, and you'll only know that if you're the inviteable type. Usually it's in one of the Upper houses (the sixteen-to-eighteen-year-olds: Stables for the girls, Lake for the guys): whoever got lucky enough to bag one of the bigger double bedrooms and has a roomie who doesn't mind people being sick in their bed. It's the thing everyone will be talking about tomorrow. It's the gossip text-book for the whole term.

And I'm at it. We're at it.

UM.

WOT?

This is not standard Heidi protocol. The Finch isn't exactly your average school, but it has its cliques, its little groups. The druggie kids in bands, the alky kids in bands, the Ana girls, the We Hate Everything crowd. Our cheerleaders are cutters with credit cards and police cautions, but it's no different from any other school once you slice past the extra cash. Same rules everywhere. And the rules say that weird-ass Leftover Squad Lower Schoolies do not get to play with the grown-up toys. Maybe Ludo might have sneaked in last year, back when she hung with the Pill Popettes. Maybe even goomy loomy Fili, when she was an emo. But never Big Dai, the fat gay kid in the corner. And definitely never me, the faculty brat, that freak with the braids, the girl who only ever hears about this stuff the next morning, after the Mothership's driven me back up the hill.

Maybe I've been watching too much *Mycroft Christie Investigates* lately, but it's possible there's a hole in the fabric of time and space, responsible for our being here.

The room is filling up now, starting to get crowded and stuffy. Bottles and cans of Coke get passed to the corner by the window, where, under cover of an armchair, Brendan Wilson tops them up from a glass bottle. Packets of Doritos fly overhead. Jo-Jo Bemelmans brings in a stack of pizza boxes, and the smell of cheese and garlic takes over from the icky mix of perfume and hairspray. Scheherezade Adams swans in, all bounce and straps and brand-new nose.

I think about sneaking out, but Ludo's squeaking next to me, eyes big, reeling off a list of names under her breath like a butler at some fancy soiree. She's got her hand wrapped round my wrist, squeezing whenever someone especially significant goes by. It's not so bad, I suppose. I'm out of the habit of being squished in with so many other people, but really it's not that different from watching TV, in smell-o-vision. And I'm in the perfect location to play detective. I'll observe the Finch species in its natural habitat: monitor behavioral patterns, take notes.

Timo Januscz is drinking alone.

Flick Henshall has reportedly locked herself in the second floor loo in Stables. (Are these two facts related?)

Honey Prentiss has broken her arm, which may prevent her from playing the oboe all term. (Scheherezade looks quite pleased.)

Miyu Sugawara wants Oliver Bass to know that someone is a bitch, very loudly, just at one of those moments when the room falls oddly quiet. (Note: Anna-Louise Darbyshire's ULife photo page has been an impressive array of kissy-face snog photos all summer, none of them featuring Oliver.)

And there are the newbies to check out, too: the ones who were just pretty or booze-equipped enough to get the McCartney Party auto-approval. A new Ana girl. Some guy with peroxide hair, a military greatcoat, and piercings on his piercings, trying to eat pizza without snagging mozzarella on his spikes. A skinny boy all in black Fili's gone to talk to by the window, as if Goth radar is yanking them together, though actually he looks sort of familiar.

There's another new girl I almost miss, from the crowd around her, then from how almost invisible she is in person. She's pale and gaunt and angular, arms and legs folded up and sticking out like some sort of insect, and wearing the sort of makeup that looks like it isn't makeup. I hear someone say "model." It computes.

"OH MY GOD," breathes Ludo. "Yuliya Kusnetsova? She's, like, EVERYWHERE. She did, like, *Vogue Italia* two months ago? She's HUGE."

She's kind of the opposite, but I let it slide. The name's familiar anyway.

"I think she's Fili's new roommate," I say. "They've got that big double on the top floor of Manor, upstairs from you?"

Ludo gets her death grip onto my wrist again.

"NO! Oh. My. God. Seriously? OH MY GOD. That is . . ."

"Awesome?" I suggest.

"TOTALLY!"

Somehow I'm not sure Fili will be so keen. But before I can drag her away from Gothboy to ask, I feel a tug on one of my braids, and then nearly fly off the sofa as a body leaps over from behind and drops into the empty space beside me.

"Ding ding, Ryder. All aboard."

Big Dai Wyn Davies: man mountain, king of the bear hug. Well, what's left of him. Dai didn't get to be Big Dai just from being six foot four, and it looks as if he's going to need a new nickname. Same stupid grin, same rubbish spiky blond haircut, entirely new body.

"Holy crap, Dai, the lions really did eat you."

He looks stupidly pleased. "Safari diet. Followed by masochistic gym torture." He flexes an arm at me. Bits of it stick out, in a manner that is probably meant to be impressive.

"WHOA!" says Ludo, leaning over me to poke his biceps. "Personal trainer?"

"Yep. On whom I had the most pathetic crush, so, hello, dedication! You likey?"

Ludo gives him a small round of applause. I wrinkle my nose.

"You look like someone Photoshopped your head onto a lifeguard."

"I'll take that as the compliment you *obviously* intended it to be. *Betch*. You're looking majestic yourself, by the way. Loving the coat."

"Detective," I explain, waiting for the penny to drop. Dai's even more of a Mycroft Christie fangirl than I am.

"Oh yeah? Like that guy off the telly, right? God, can you believe how much time we wasted last year, watching that crap?" He chuckles, shaking his head. "We were such dorks."

I look down at myself. The Coat has started to seem a bit more bizarre now there are quite so many other people here to see it. In fact, now I'm paying a bit more attention, everyone else seems to be dressed a teensy bit more appropriately for a party. Not just the Upper kids who always look like that, all swingy hair and glitter makeup for 9 A.M. Biology, either. I mean *everyone*.

Fili doesn't count: Aside from her being crazy-beautiful already, it is Goth Law never to be seen without the uniform and the face. And Ludo is always perky, and pretty, and strung about with jingly sparkly things. But she's different somehow: just a few slim gold threads around her wrists and neck instead of that ever-increasing cuff of grubby neon plastic bangles she had last year, golden streaks in her smooth dark hair, red lips instead of peachy-pink. Dai's got new threads to go with his new absence of stomach, too: magenta polo shirt with the collar flipped up, low-slung jeans so there's a wide line of boxers showing. He's even wearing man-jewelry: some tourist junk from his holiday, beads with a bit hanging down shaped like a tooth.

Pod people.

My friends have been replaced by Pod people. Robots. Zombie doppelgängers from space. The Leftover Squad has been hijacked by evil clones, and we haven't even been given our first mission yet.

OK, rewind that thought. I have no moral objection to people looking nice. I might not be exactly managing it myself, in my baggy jeans and my superdork braids, but that just makes me the poster child for not being fooled by the advertising: It's what's inside that counts, don't judge a book, etc. It's what comes with the extra layers of lipgloss and perfume that's spooking me. Ludo finally lets go of my wrist, but only to do a quick hitch-and-jiggle on her bra, tugging her vest top down a notch as she eyes Scheherezade. Dai's telling me some story about lost luggage on the way to Madagascar, but the whole time he's looking around, eyes sliding up and down, approving and disapproving. Even Fili is tinkering with her millions of long dark braids, eyelashes fluttering shyly as Gothboy tries on her favorite ring with the spider on it.

It's catching. Everyone's doing it. I don't think there's a person in the room actually enjoying themselves: They're too busy checking each other out.

Not me, though: The eyes hit, connect, and slide on by.

Maybe my fledgling detective geekiness is not so attractive. Maybe I've got the casting for the Leftover Squad all wrong. I'm the comedy sidekick who falls in poo. The talking dog. The redshirt who gets killed off in episode 4, and no one really minds.

"This is SO awesome," whispers Ludo loudly in my ear.

OAR.

SUM.

I nog: nod and shrug, both at once.

Half an hour later, with the sky dark outside and nothing but MTV on the plasma screen to light the room, I realize I'm not dealing with zombie robot doppelgängers. It's the love potion episode. Every TV show has it sooner or later. Magic spell, monster bite, something in the water: romantic Kryptonite that makes people lick faces with people they shouldn't. Mycroft Christie ended up snogging a vampire, an evil old lady who trained exploding hamsters to break into banks, and Jori Song (twice) while under the influence of bad mojo. Hilarious consequences generally ensue.

It's not so entertaining when you're in the middle of it.

OK, there's not exactly a Roman orgy happening. People are still wearing clothes, so far as I can tell from the flicker of the TV. It's prewatershed, family-friendly, PG-13. But everywhere I look, it's going on. Tongues and hands and giggles in corners. Oliver Bass is proving how over Anna-Louise he is by sticking his tongue down Miyu's throat. Scheherezade is sitting on Jo-Jo's lap, arms draped over his shoulders. Brendan Wilson is sliding a hand up the new Ana girl's thigh, while she coyly smiles and fiddles with the hem of her skirt.

I hear Fili's laugh over the music, and see her curled up and cozy with her boy twin, holding hands, shoulders pressed together. I go to nudge Ludo, and realize she's otherwise occupied, the peroxide-haired, pierced newbie guy's mouth on hers, his hand resting, as if by total accident, on her boob. I squint my left eye closed, trying not to look, but I can still hear a vague slurpy noise. I turn to grab Dai, but the seat next to me is empty. I finally spot him in the corner near the door, dancing with Henry Kim and looking like he's won the lottery (which he kind of has, in Finch Gay Quarter terms: Henry Kim is famously the triple threat of cute, rich, and smart, and Dai has been lusting from afar as long as I've known him).

The Coat suddenly feels too appropriate, in all the wrong ways. I'm an accidental perv, trapped here staring at a roomful of people getting it on, because there's not really anywhere else to look. The only other person in the room who isn't coupling up (or trying to) is Model Yuliya, who is yawning over her can of Diet Coke and flicking through a magazine.

I check my watch. I begged and pleaded until the Mothership promised I could stay until 9:30 tonight. It's only just after 8.

I remember my Bubble Wrap bag's at my feet. Betsy lent me an Agatha Christie novel, so I could practice my detecting skills. Maybe now would be a good time to whip out Agatha and read?

OK, that's *definitely* not the strangely attractive kind of geekiness.

I could go and find Dad Man, in his little cubbyhole of an office. The Mothership might have finished setting up down at the pool already: She could leave early, take me back down the hill to my poky little attic bedroom. I could watch the *Mycroft Christie Investigates* season 3 finale again, in bed, with that Snickers bar that I sneaked into the shopping trolley while the Mothership was fussing over whether bananas counted as Amber on her Traffic Light diet regime.

I reach down for my bag to get my phone, and when I come back up, the seat next to me is no longer empty. Etienne Gracey. He's a Shroom, or he was: one of the Lower

School bands, though he must be Upper School now. They played at the End of Year Ball. He sang.

"You're Heidi, yeah?" he says, shouting, over the music. He's leaning in very close.

"Etienne, right?"

He smiles, nodding. I can see a little frost of stubble on his chin and his upper lip, glowing blue, then pink in the video light. I feel something touch my back, and try not to jump. It's his arm, sliding along the back of the sofa.

"Let me get you a drink," he says, and the arm disappears from my back.

"Oh My God Heidi!" whispers Ludo in my ear, apparently coming up for air. "You are SO lucky! He's, like, so TOTALLY gorgeous."

I suppose he is. I mean, he's not as pretty as Little Leaf Teddy. Not anywhere near as pretty as Mycroft Christie. But he's sort of a Finch pinup. He's dated Scheherezade. And now he's settling back onto the couch next to me, pressing a can of Coke into my hand and sliding his arm back into position.

Ludo's elbow jabbing me excitedly in the rib area is not helping me to get my brain around this scenario, but Peroxide Guy distracts her again with a little more casual hand/boob interfacing, and it's like we're alone together, me and Etienne.

Heidi and Etienne.

Is this how it works, then? You just kind of sit there, and

wait for some boy to turn up and kiss you? I've been serving cups of tea to nice old ladies all summer: This all feels ultra-weird. But I suppose it's OK. It'll get it out of the way. I'm not fourteen anymore. I'm fifteen. This is what fifteen-year-olds do.

I take a sip out of my can, and try not to cough as the whatever-it-is goes down. I don't really do alcohol. I'm probably drunk already.

"Thanks," I say, tilting the can at him.

Etienne just nods, bobbing his head slightly as the music changes. Madonna thrusts her scary manlegs at me, in a not-especially-sexy kind of way.

I drink some more, in case my mouth tastes of anything weird. Because Etienne's going to kiss me. I think. I wonder if he'll feel prickly. I suppose he is quite pretty, up close.

Maybe you don't just sit there and wait? I didn't see anyone else having trouble getting to the kissing part of the evening, but I'm definitely doing something wrong. Talking, maybe? Are we supposed to that first?

"So . . . any new Shrooms songs since last year?"

"Shrooms? We split. Creative differences, you know? I'm working on some solo material now, though." He snarls at the TV screen. "Real music, y'know?"

"Mhmm," I say into my Coke. "I'd love to hear it. Some-time. If you'd like?"

"Yeah?" He keeps bobbing his head. "Cool."

The ultraweird keeps on growing. I think I just asked him on a date, sort of. This is not standard behavior. This is not

Heidi. There actually really truly is love potion floating in the air, making everyone moronic, and I am not immune after all.

"So, your Dad is, like, the security guy at night, yeah?"

"Night porter, yep." I try a goofy shrug. "Kind of embarrassing."

"What? Oh, yeah, I guess. Anyway, me and the guys were wondering: Could you, like, distract him tonight or something?"

I look up, and see "the guys" hovering behind Etienne, looking hopeful. Big looming Upper Schoolers from Lake: Dave something, Jules Harper, some guy I don't know at all.

"The *real* McCartney party's supposed to be up in Toni's room in Stables, only she says your Dad was, like, patrolling all over down there, so we ended up down here with the kiddies in Baby House." He waves his can at the room, eye-rolling. "No offense."

I swallow a big gulp, and taste the whatever-it-is, sticky on my teeth.

"No offense, yep," I mumble.

"So, could you, like, go pretend to be ill or something, just to, like, keep him busy or whatever?"

He leans in again, arm still round my shoulder, fingers just lightly stroking the top of my arm.

"Sure," I hear myself say. "Whatever."

"Awesome."

He gives my arm a squeeze, hops off the sofa, and he and "the guys" vanish.

OAK.

HEY.

Emergency Protocol #4. Ejector seats engaged. Alert, alert, incoming. When I say run, run.

I fumble for my bag, but Ludo's amazing ability to get her face snogged off and still see what's going on next to her is still in place. Her hand closes round my wrist again. I pull away, vaguely shaking my head, and climb over various writhey wriggly arms and legs to get out, out into the corridor.

It's cool and bright. No sweaty people, no stinky pizza, just a nice ordinary school-like corridor, with a notice board about netball practice times and when the nurse will be available. The real world, back where I know the rules.

Ludo bangs the door on the unreal world of the common room, and scoots up to dangle off my shoulder, eyes like two fried eggs.

"Oh My God, what WAS that? I mean, WHAT? I mean, OH MY GOD!"

"Ryder, baby, what gives?"

Not-So-Big Dai appears, his face pink, a huge smile on his face, Henry close behind him.

"I KNOW! He was, like, all over her, and then FOOM, GONE."

"Etienne Gracey. Heidi, you *turned down* Etienne Gracey. That's . . . that's a parallel universe." Dai remembers Henry lingering at his shoulder. "Sorry. I didn't mean . . ."

Henry shrugs. "It's Etienne Gracey. No offense, but I'm right there with you."

Ludo grins her tiny pearly grin at me. Then her eyes suddenly get wider. Huge. Fried eggs times twenty. She starts swatting her hands, slapping her palms against me and Dai like we're on fire, and making little squeaks.

"OH MY GOD. I get it. I totally get it. Don't you get it?"

Dai looks at Henry. They don't get it.

I don't get it either. So much for my fledgling detective skills.

"DUH! Only possible explanation? She's totally SEEING someone already."

Dai gasps. Actually gasps.

"No!"

"TOTALLY. Right, Heidi? Right?"

Before I can get a word out, Ludo wraps her arms around my tummy and hugs me so hard I feel my elbows click. Dai joins in, pressing my head into his shirt. Henry wraps a cashmere-clad arm round me, too, even though I don't really know him well enough for hugging, and the three of them squish me even tighter, with Ludo making small "eee" noises and jumping up and down.

"Anything of interest?"

They break off. Fili's leaning on the wall, Gothboy just behind, looking bemused.

"Ryder here has just turned down the tongue services of one Etienne Gracey, on account of having — drumroll please — a secret boyfriend."

Ludo nods her head superfast, mouth wide open.

Fili quirks a brow. "Seriously?"

I look at Ludo, lipstick smeared into a doughnut round her mouth. I look at Dai, Henry's hand resting ever so casually on Dai's belt. I look at Fili, and how close Gothboy is standing, fingers twining in hers.

New season. New lineup. *Leftover Squad: The Boyfriend Years*. No room for Frog Girls here.

Well, honestly, what would you do?

Recipe for an Imaginary Boyfriend

INGREDIENTS:

A name

A haircut

Eyes (two, of improbable color: seafoam green, topaz, etc.)

Stylish yet attainable clothing

An adorable "How We Met" anecdote

Reasons why he is loveable

Reasons why he thinks I am loveable

Reasons why he is very far away and unlikely to phone me up

Hobbies (NOT SCRABBLE)

METHOD:

• Procure ingredients from Heidibrain.

• Watch lots of *Mycroft Christie Investigates* for valuable insight into boylike behavior.

• Shape the mixture into vague appearance of Monsieur Le Sexay (exact biological accuracy not required — let's not even go there).

• Snog (imaginarily).

"An imaginary boyfriend?" Betsy breathes in through her nose. "OK. That's . . . uh . . ."

"The most amazingly brilliant idea in the history of the universe?"

"I was going to say 'creative,' honeypie. But hey, he's your imaginary lovemonkey. Maybe you've seen a side to him I'm missing."

It's the Saturday after the first week of school, and I'm back in my apron, playing waitress at the Little Leaf café. If the Finch is one step sideways from normal, then the Little Leaf is a bus ride away. If you don't look too closely, it's a perfect picture-postcard tearoom on the village green. It sells homemade scones with jam and clotted cream, twenty-four different kinds of tea, and only one kind of coffee (instant and horrible), and there are still lacy tablecloths on half of the tables. There's even a shelf running round the ceiling displaying novelty teapots in the shape of red London buses. Traditional British Hospitality.

Only Betsy is American, with her own take on what counts as "traditional."

So the walls are tangerine, sky blue, and pink — one of each, with a dusty black wall behind the counter that we use as a chalkboard for the day's specials, Teddy's daft little doodles of customers, and the Daily Wisdom: SMILE! IT MAKES ME REMEMBER TO WASH MY HANDS BEFORE SERVING YOU. EAT A CAKE! OR THE KITTEN DIES. There are squashy sofas and armchairs infiltrating their way between the lace tablecloths. The shelf with the buses also has dragons, a bust of Shakespeare with a red plastic clown nose, and a selection of novelty hats, from Deerstalker to Top. There's even a picture of the Queen (and you can only see the felt-pen moustache if you stand on a chair).

Tourists eat it up. Tourists take photos of themselves pointing at the menu. Locals go to the Big Bean coffeehouse opposite for venti mochas.

I still smile every time I walk through the door anyway. Betsy's been the provider of sanity (and cake) all summer. If anyone's going to understand the logic of my sudden need for an imaginary boyfriend, I reckon it's her.

She slides a trayload of scones and tea across the counter, and I dutifully deliver it to a concertina-spined elderly couple by the Little Leaf window. The place is deadsville again: September is back-to-school time for the tourists, too. It's raining. Even the Daily Wisdom (TODAY'S MUFFINS ARE ROUND FLAT BREADY THINGS: *THOSE OTHER ONES ARE JUST CUPCAKES WITH EGOS*) seems a bit glum. The first week back in Finchworld hasn't been a breeze, either. Mr. Prowse has already rejected my Poem on an Autumn Leaf homework and demanded I do it again for next week, on pain of being reported to Mrs. Kemble, the Demon Headmistress. The Mothership's decided we're on a Red Foods Only phase on the Traffic Light diet, now Dad Man's back to sleeping up at the Finch six nights a week and isn't around to demand fish fingers and chips. The post-McCartney Party fallout is still ongoing, what with

Etienne Gracey glaring at me for failure to distract, Jo-Jo Bemelmans getting busted with a pillowcase full of empty vodka bottles, and Flick Henshall having ended up in a clinic after having her stomach pumped. Dad Man had to drive her out there at 4 in the morning. He looked all stringy the next day. I'm sworn to secrecy, of course, which in reality means I have to sit there pretending I know nothing while everyone else talks about it, because Flick Henshall does this about twice a term, and her completely empty bedroom is sort of a giveaway. Basically, my own parents are making me lie. No wonder I'm entering the subterfuge business.

And then there's . . . the other stuff.

"We going to have the company of the gang from up on the hill today?" Betsy asks, dusting invisible crumbs off the green velvet sofa, as if that'll magically make some customers appear on it.

"Not sure if they'll make it, actually. They're all pretty busy. With, you know, homework. And . . . things."

Betsy peers out at me from beneath her hair, narrows her eyes, and pointedly sets us up with a large pot of English Breakfast.

"Feeling a little left behind, hon?" she says gently.

OK, maybe not that good. She's a bit clever, Betsy.

"It's just not how I pictured the first week back, that's all."

I'm being an idiot, I know it. It's not as if over the summer my little room magically flew five miles closer to school, so I could spend my evenings being exposed to Bad Influences and Extreme Teenage Behaviors like everyone else, and come home at curfew on the Bike o' Doom, by myself. And we hadn't actually made *plans* to watch kittens on YouTube when everyone got back. Fili never promised to be perching on the end of the balance beam at the end of every day, waiting to lend me an earbud. We're still hanging out, like we used to, kind of: the Leftover Squad, plus extras. *I am not Frog Girl.*

I pick up the tufty end of my left braid, and glare at it. "It's like everyone else got a different script, you know? And I'm having to make it up as I go."

"Including a boyfriend?"

"Including a boyfriend. And don't look at me like that! It's not because I'm jealous. I think it's nice that all my friends have hooked up with people. They're happy, I'm happy."

That part is totally true. Dai's so giddy about having snagged Henry he keeps walking into doorframes. Ludo is even squeakier than usual over her Peroxide Eric. Fili and Gothboy float around in matching outfits (and since Gothboy has turned out to be Simon Grove, who last year was a wispy blond guy in a "Jesus Saves" T-shirt who used to fall asleep a lot in Biology, his transformation into her perfect twin seems like some extraspecial romantic gesture). It's kind of amusing to observe.

Betsy's still looking unconvinced.

"I'm just mucking about, honest. It's not like I set out to make up a boyfriend. Ludo got the wrong idea: I didn't put her right. Actually it's pretty entertaining, working out what he should be like. Like...pick 'n' mix. Only with body parts."

She's smirking now. "OK, honey, I'll buy it. I wish my first boyfriend had been imaginary. Then I could go ahead and unimagine him again. Along with the acne, and the poison breath, and the creepy kid sister who used to stare in at us through his car window..."

"See? This is why it's the most amazing idea ever. Imaginary Boy is not going to have any of those."

After all, I am kind of an expert at this. I've been having imaginary boyfriends since I learned how to turn on a TV. So far, I've had theoretical romantic shenanigans with:

The Milkybar Kid (I was eight. He was (a) equivalent
   to me on the dorkage scale and (b) had chocolate:
   (b) was totally the clincher)
The kilt-wearing man on the porridge oats advert
   (KILT! No further explanation required)
Carson Kressley (*sigh*)
Peter from off of Narnia
Ellen Page (obligatory girl crush)
Peter Petrelli (shirtless)
MYCROFT CHRISTIE ♥

I'm practically a slut. Etienne Gracey would probably turn me down all over again, due to my intimidating sexual prowess.

"So, does he have a name? Because 'Imaginary Boy' is kind of a giveaway, hon."

"Still working on it."

Names are surprisingly tricky. All of the good ones are taken. And I can hardly call him Mycroft. I don't think my imagination is up to fake-dating a Mycroft, let alone anyone else's.

"Anything but Rupert!" comes a muffled voice from the kitchen.

Teddy. Teddy, who is usually still asleep at this hour of the morning (apparently, occasionally, I may have noticed in passing), creating his beautiful extra-fluffy curly bed hair. Fabulous tousled Teddy, seventeen-year-old god of baking, who is apparently not asleep, but in the kitchen, listening to my pathetic lack of a life.

ODE.

EAR.

I don't know why I'm embarrassed: Teddy's quite aware of how hopeless I am already. He's seen me doing sweaty karaoke to Katrina and the Waves at closing time cleanup, after all. And anyway, I happen to know he's a Teddy who is secretly not a Teddy at all, but a Rupert. (Betsy thought it sounded like a nice British name, until they moved here, and found out it translates locally as "hit me, hard, many times." There aren't even any Ruperts at the Finch. So: Rupert, Rupert Bear, Teddy.) He's kind of touchy about it. If he wants to start a mockery war, I have ammunition.

"I've got an outstanding 'How We Met' anecdote all

mapped out, though," I say, quickly, because Betsy's starting to look unconvinced. "Can you check it for plot holes? Because Ludo's starting to invent her own version, and I'm running out of enigmatic coy looks."

"Have at it," she says, pouring more tea.

I settle myself on the stool, and take a deep breath.

"OK, so, we met at Paddington station. Buying gummy bears. I mean, I was buying gummy bears. Only I was running late, and I heard the train arrive so I ran for it, and I must've left my purse in the shop when I did, because just as I was about to get on the train, someone grabbed my arm. And he was all breathless because he'd been running to catch up with me, so he couldn't get the words out to say, 'Here is your purse,' and then the train doors went BEEP BEEP BEEP and closed, and the train left, and we both just stood there. And he went, 'You missed your train,' and I went, 'Nnnnnnnngh,' because he was all tall, dark, and leather-jackety. And holding my purse, which is the purple felt one with the flower on it that's falling off a bit. So he gave it back to me, and I said, 'Thank you,' and probably our fingers brushed together with sparks of electricity, though I might skip that bit? And we just stood there, on this train platform, just the two of us. So I offered him a gummy bear and he said, 'Only if I can have a red one, they're the best,' and I said I liked the green ones best anyway, and then we just carried on talking, and la la la snogs, the end."

I take a big swig of tea.

"So, what do you think?"

"Adorable," says Betsy. "A little too adorable, maybe? But hey, that's what fantasies are for, right?"

"I could ditch the gummy bears?"

"I like the gummy bears. Nice detail."

"The ending needs a little work."

"Yeah, but still, it's a good beginning. *Love* the leather jacket."

"OK, stop, I can't take any more!"

Teddy appears in the kitchen doorway, tousled bed hair in place (lightly dusted with flour), apron on over the top of stripy pajama trousers and monster-feet slippers.

"Nobody's going to give a crap about the leather jacket and the gummy bears," he says, wagging a spoon at us and dripping icing on the floor, "not when the rest of it doesn't make any sense. Heidi, if you left your purse in the shop, how did you get through the turnstile onto the platform? Are you at Paddington *train* station or *underground* station? What are you even doing in London? I mean, don't you have somewhere to go? Doesn't he? And seriously, if some strange guy steals your purse and grabs your arm at a train station, you want to push him onto the tracks, not kiss him. Just a suggestion."

He grabs the chalk, doodles a gummy bear with a sad face on the wall, and heads back to the kitchen with a grin.

"My son, the death of romance," sighs Betsy.

"Nope, he's right. It's not exactly realistic, is it?"

I decide not to mention the previous draft versions I came up with in Chemistry, when I was meant to be doing experimental things with potassium permanganate. There were pirates. And giraffe riding. And he had a beret.

Apparently imaginary boyfriend–construction is harder than it looks.

"Maybe you should keep it simple," Betsy offers. "There don't need to be fireworks. Just go with something you'll be able to remember. Something familiar, you know?"

I spend the total lack of a lunchtime rush contemplating alternative locations for Imaginary Boy to share my gummy bears. Then I decide he (Michael?) is a vegetarian, and so we strike up a conversation about how gummy bears contain bits of dead cow. Then I decide that discussing bits of dead cow is probably not the ideal date conversation, and actually that he (Mikhail) is kind of a jerk for even mentioning it, in fact, ruining my gummy bears. And who does he (Mickey) even think he (Mikey) is, coming and hassling me in the park?

By the end of the day, I've dumped him (Artemis) about seventeen times, before we've even properly met. And he still doesn't have a name that isn't stupid.

"Inspiration for you," says Betsy as we close up early, sliding me a paper bag along with the little brown envelope of cash that I really obviously haven't earned.

"What's this?"

I peer inside the bag and find a warm, solid gingerbread man; his iced-on eyes and buttons still slightly soft.

Betsy looks innocent.

"The Perfect Boyfriend. And he's not even imaginary."

Boarding school Dining Halls are not what you imagine. I've seen six, and I can tell you now: Forget what the pictures in the brochures say, and put all Hogwarty thoughts from your mind. There will be no mahogany paneling, or portraits of old dead guys, or feasting on roasted wild boar by candlelight. The Finch Dining Hall is strip-lit, smells of beans, and looks a bit like a posh McDonald's. The food is just as enticing: Oil Pie, Lettuce in Soup, and the ever-popular Armored Pizza. (If the Mothership's Red Peppers stuffed with Red Lentils, Red Onion, and Red Cabbage don't kill me, their Fish Surprise will.)

I used to have other reasons to hate lunchtimes, obviously. Arrive in the middle of a term? You're already screwed, because every little gang has already planted an invisible flag on their own table. Occasionally cause the Mothership, aka Mrs. Ryder the PE Witch, to come over "just to see how you're doing, babes?" No one's going to offer you that spare seat. Get a reputation for potentially coming to lunch with a half-dissected amphibian attached to your bag?

WELD.

UH.

Fortunately, these days I have my pre-reserved spot just like everyone else, so I line up with my plastic tray and shuffle through the line. There's not a lot left, and somehow I end up with nothing but four different kinds of potato on my plate by the time I've made it through the toxic food sludge. I grab an apple (green, just to add to my Traffic Light rebellion), then weave through the tables, following the sound of Ludo's giggles.

Our official Leftover Squad corner is looking a little crowded these days, even with Ludo sitting on Peroxide Eric's lap, wrapped up in the ends of his military coat, and Fili and Simon sitting so close together they might as well be sharing one chair.

"Ryder!" shouts Dai, waving me over. "At long last. We were starting to think you'd turned into the invisible woman."

Henry stands at once, and offers me his seat.

"Isn't that the mysterious Yuliya's job?" he asks, lounging against the back of Dai's chair, while Dai beams with pride.

Yuliya, the stick insect Russian model, has managed to not turn up to a single class I'm in so far. I'm starting to think I imagined her, too.

"OH MY GOD, like, leave her alone?" Ludo flicks her hair, not noticing that some of it is now tangled in Peroxide Eric's nose ring. "She probably has to sleep a lot to maintain her complexion."

"She's not going to come in here anyway," says Dai, hovering a hand over my plate, and deciding to steal my apple instead. "Models don't eat. Well, not food."

I waggle Potato Variety #1: The Soggy Chip at him. "Don't think this qualifies."

"That is SO stereotypical," says Ludo, swinging her hair again.

There's a faint groan from behind her. I wince on Peroxide Eric's behalf. He gives me a grateful grin, as he disentangles himself.

The Mothership has instructed me not to be friends with "the new boy with all the metal in his face," but then she says that about everyone. So far, he seems to be sitting back and observing Finchworld with a kind of bemused smile, and I can get behind that.

"I'm just saying, she's probably got her reasons, which are probably, like, none of our business? And she's Fili's new roomie, you know? So we should TOTALLY be making her feel welcome."

"Very true," says Dai, through a mouthful of apple. "So what *is* she like, then?"

We all look at Fili.

Fili patters her fingertips on the table, and narrows her eyes. Then she seems to notice that everyone's staring, hanging on her words. "She's . . . tall," she says eventually.

We wait, but that seems to be all we're getting.

(I understand, though. She means: *I think things I don't want to say right now.* Fili-code isn't so hard to follow once you know her. Sometimes she likes to work things out in her head properly before committing them to the open air, that's all. She can come out with whole paragraphs when it's just us two, swinging our legs on the balance beam. We still haven't got around to doing that yet this term, but, hey, it's been busy, with the new classes, and settling in, and Simon. There's not really room for three of us out there.)

"Simon? Anything you'd like to add? Like, actual information of some kind?" says Dai.

Simon frowns, and says slowly, "She has really big hands."

"Ladies and gentlemen, the Finch gossip scandal of the year."

"Unless there's a thrilling story about how he found out she has really big hands?" suggests Henry, nudging Dai with his elbow.

Simon frowns again, blinking apologetically at Fili through his wispy black hair. "I just . . . looked?"

Fili pats his hand, reassuringly, and he looks a bit less terrified. It's sort of adorable, how puppylike he is.

Dai sighs heavily. "It's so worthwhile, knowing the people with the inside scoop."

"She's doing PAG," says Fili, softly.

"OH MY GOD!" squeaks Ludo, eliciting another pained grunt from Peroxide Eric as he rubs ruefully at his ear. "Really? That's so awesome! We'll be, like, best friends! There'll probably be press photographers coming to see it and everything!"

I stab a lump in my gray mash. "PAG?"

"Performing Arts Group," says Henry. "We put on the Wassail show? With Venables?"

I nod. Everyone was still talking about the Wassail show when I arrived last January. It's the Christmas play, really, but the Finch likes to think it's progressive and embraces all cultures (as long as they can pay the fees), so they can't call it that. There are still photos all over the music rooms of the Main Hall set up with the posh auditorium seating that sort of folds out of the walls, with Henry in a purple cloak peering out from behind a curtain, and Big Dai dressed up as the Cowardly Lion. Dai looks more like a Cowardly Koala, but there's a Tin Man and a Scarecrow and Gillian Gerhardt in gingham, so I'm assuming the continental detour was an accident. And I know Venables, even though I've managed to escape his classes so far. He's got a little love posse who follow him round adoringly, and quite possibly leave apples on his desk. Even the Mothership's always going on about how hilarious he is in the staff room. I don't really get it. All I see is one of those teachers who wears skinny jeans even though he's going bald, wants everyone to call him Phil, and likes to sit cross-legged on the floor so he can "feel the vibe, man."

"Auditions, next Wednesday," says Dai.

"Can you believe there were only, like, TWENTY places on the sheet for the Lower School? And you just KNOW that Scheherezade Adams was going to put herself down for, like, ALL of them."

"But, Mr. Venables!" lisps Henry, tilting his head into a scarily accurate impersonation, only with a bit less cleavage. "It simply wouldn't be fair on the people who've bought tickets if I didn't play heroine and hero! It's *so* much modern that way."

"Don't worry, Ryder, I signed us all up."

Peroxide Eric sweeps Ludo's hair aside, and raises a hand. "Not me. Not exactly my scene."

It's not exactly my scene, either. I give good audience. I am well trained in the art of viewing. Participation, not so much.

But maybe that's the old Heidi talking. I'm Heidi-with-a-boyfriend. Heidi-with-a-boyfriend could be in a play.

"They have non-speaking roles," says Fili, softly.

"Scenery, lighting, music . . ." Dai has his best encouraging face on.

"Costume!" bellows Ludo, tugging on The Coat gleefully and nearly yanking my head off.

I squish down the tiny inner mumble of disappointment that even Heidi-with-a-boyfriend is not expected to wow the school with her undiscovered acting talent. A good detective should be watching from the wings anyway. It's like Mycroft Christie says in episode 1.11, "Noises Off": *One can't see who's pulling the strings if one is one of the puppets.*

Dai's phone beeps. "Sorry, kiddies, must fly," he says, chucking my half-eaten apple back on my tray. "The weights room is calling. Time to get sweaty."

Henry smirks, and murmurs something in Dai's ear.

"You can't go now!" Ludo's bobbing about on Peroxide Eric's knee, like a five-year-old who needs a wee. "I know a thing about the thing!"

Fili glances at me, then gives her a stern look. "Ludo?"

"We're not talking about the thing," says Dai sternly. "The

thing is none of our business, remember? Unless the thingee wants to share?"

They all look at me.

"I'm a *thingee*?"

"Oh, come ON," moans Ludo, her knees jiggling up and down. "The BOY? The super-mysterious secret boyfriend? The more gorgeous than Etienne Gracey boy we're all dying to know about, WHOSE NAME I MIGHT HAPPEN TO KNOW?"

They all look intrigued. "They" includes me.

Ludo strangles me again, hauling on my collar and thrusting the inner lining of The Coat at Dai.

"HELLO? The coat OBVIOUSLY belongs to the super-mysterious secret boy, because, duh, why else would she be wearing it? And what does it say in the coat?"

Dai leans in. I crane my head around to see the neatly sewn nametape under the hanging loop that I've never really paid any attention to.

"Hartley," he reads.

"How romantic," says Henry.

Hartley. It sounds sort of familiar. I've probably seen it written there before without really noticing, the way you walk past the same row of shops all the time but couldn't put them in order without them right in front of your nose.

"So, Ryder, does Hartley have a first name, or are you two sticking with the kinky boarding school thing?"

I take a deep breath.

They continue to all stare at me.

I can't do it: not lie straight to their faces. I'm coming clean. I'm telling the truth.

We all simply want to belong.

"Ed," I say. "His name's Ed."

I have no idea where it came from: The words just pop out before I can inspect them for Paddington stationesque plot holes. But I like it. I picture the little gingerbread dude Betsy gave me. I've saved him: propped him up on my bedside table, guarding Agatha Christie.

"Aww, look, she's gone all girly," squeaks Ludo, and I realize I'm grinning.

Ed Hartley. My boyfriend's name is Ed Hartley. Gingerbread Ed.

EX.

SELL.

LEANT.

Now that he's got a name, the rest of the ingredients are going to just fall in my lap. I can feel it. I'm not just audience now. I get an executive producer credit. I'm the show runner for *Heidi!*, the heartwarming yet hilarious tale of a plucky gal and her imaginary friend (not to be confused with that thing up a mountain, with the goats).

Time for me to put my detective skills to work, starting with the basics: interrogation.

Mycroft Christie shines bright light in the eyes of the guys he's fleecing for information. I don't see why nonsentient baked people should be any different. I take the gingerbread man from his perch beside my Pinocchio alarm clock and prop him up against the base of my desk lamp. One of his eyes got a bit squished while I was bringing him home, and he's starting to look sort of sweaty, but we can put that down to my intimidating detective demeanor. He still smells delicious, though. I'd be tempted to eat him, if that didn't open up a whole can of associated dodge now that he's my boyfriend.

Interrogation #1 goes something like this:

A tiny cell. Heidi sits on her chair backward. The ginger-
bread man stays standing, due to his legs not being bendy.
HEIDI: Hello, sexy. Please inform me of your vital statistics.
GINGERBREAD MAN: (enigmatic silence)
HEIDI: OK, perhaps the "sexy" thing is a bit forward. Please don't sue me for sexual harassment?
GINGERBREAD MAN: (enigmatic silence)
HEIDI: Although, come to think of it, you are technically naked, so we're probably about even on the inappropriate behavior front.
GINGERBREAD MAN: (enigmatic silence)
HEIDI: So, what kind of music are you into? Who would win in a fight: astronauts or cavemen? Boxers or briefs?

GINGERBREAD MAN: (enigmatic silence: possible sarcastic expression)

Mycroft Christie makes this look easy. But he has a leather-clad sexy sidekick to help him. And maybe my Gingerbread Ed's like Mycroft: one of those stoic noble types, who gets tied to a chair and thumped about once a week, till he just wriggles prettily and then escapes.

Or maybe Mycroft Christie has just never tried to interrogate a gingerbread man.

OK, this is getting embarrassing.

FOE.

CUSS.

Betsy said to keep it simple. To stick to something familiar. I'm going about this all wrong: trying to come up with a brand-new imaginary person, when I can just borrow one. Trying to *be* the hero, when the hero's what I'm hunting. After all, there's one person I already know inside out and backward. And he's definitely the type to wear The Coat.

Interrogation #2:

A dimly lit penthouse, belonging to time-traveling gentleman detective Mycroft Christie. He returns home to find a young lady mixing him a cocktail. It's not his usual colleague, Jori Song, but the equally foxalicious Miss Heidi Ryder.

HEIDI: Good evening, Mycroft. I'm from the Time Bureau, here to give you your new assignment.

MYCROFT CHRISTIE: Time Bureau? Madam, there's no such thing!

HEIDI: Ooh! That's from episode 1.4, "Lost in Metropolis," the scene in the Chinese restaurant where the evil journalist woman tries to expose you. Right before you pour soup all over yourself so you can run away. I love that bit.

MYCROFT CHRISTIE: (attractive crinkly smile) It appears you know me rather well.

HEIDI: Episode 1.13, "Cavalry," when it looks like you're about to tell Jori everything, and then don't. And yes, I do know you rather well. Almost as if I'm some sort of scary obsessive fangirl with your entire life on DVD. Or something. Anyway, this new assignment. I need you to go undercover as my boyfriend.

MYCROFT CHRISTIE: I can't cook. I'm terribly afraid of the dark. I have a severe allergy to bee stings, shrimp, and unrequited love.

HEIDI: Perfect! I am taking notes. No quoting from season 3 allowed, though. That's when you grew The Horrible Beard. Ed can't have a Horrible Beard.

MYCROFT CHRISTIE: When I was just a little older than you, I fell off my hoverbike and broke my leg in three places.

HEIDI: No hoverbikes, either.

MYCROFT CHRISTIE: I was nursed back to health by the most charming young woman.

HEIDI: Bingo! I smell a potential "How We Met" anecdote! You're pretty good at this. Anymore?

THE MOTHERSHIP: Hi, babes!

MYCROFT CHRISTIE: (breaks chair over her head for interrupting)

HEIDI: Er. Don't do that. Well, do, but not right now?

We're not in a penthouse. I'm not foxalicious. And the Mothership is looking at me kind of funny, which is fair enough, because I'm probably all pink-faced and ridiculous-looking, what with the talking to people who aren't there.

"I'm . . . rehearsing. For the Performing Arts Group. Auditions. This week?"

Actually, that's quite impressive as explanations go. She seems pleased anyway.

"That's great, babes! Be nice to have you getting a bit more involved in school activities. Not stuck up here watching telly all the time."

I nog.

"I'll leave you to it, babes," she says, backing out. Then her eyes fall on the desk. The lamp. The gingerbread man, standing there trying to look innocent.

I think the Mothership just caught my boyfriend hiding in my bedroom. I feel so grown-up.

"Hei-di," she says, with a sigh. "I know you and your father think it's a bit silly, but it does help me to stick to it if you do it, too, and I don't think he really fits my Traffic Light system, does he?"

"Well, no. But I haven't eaten him. He's . . . my inspiration. If I suddenly feel an urge for naughty Yellow foods on a Red day, I'll know he's watching. So just leave him there, yeah? Don't tidy him up or anything."

She smooths her hand down one of my braids, tucking in the straggly bits, and makes one of those cutesy Mothership faces: tilt head, sigh.

"Everything all right, babes? Anything you want to tell me?"

I do want to tell her. *I've got this amazing boyfriend, called Ed, who smells like cinnamon and looks like Mycroft Christie, and I don't even care how weird it is, because just thinking about him makes me smile, just like Dai does when he talks about Henry, and Ludo does whenever Peroxide Eric sweeps into a room, and Fili and Simon do all the time, because they're never apart. Maybe even better than that. And I belong, properly belong, and I'll never be Frog Girl again.*

But she's the Mothership. She understands the rules of netball, but I don't think she's qualified to deal with Ed.

And anyway, I don't have to. I've got Gingerbread Ed, my little sentry on the desk, keeping all my secrets safe.

Now Ed's got a name and a face (I'm picturing a little more Mycroft than Gingerbread Man, though a bit younger, obviously), life is sweet. Now I'm primed to giggle along in any conversation, ready to throw in a casual little detail from my own love life. I'll have to do some editing, obviously, if anyone asks: Mycroft Christie's life tends to involve a few more fistfights with evil ninjas than the average not-on-television person's does. Our first official date was a movie (though killer vampire bats didn't fly off the screen and start attacking people when me and Ed did it). I've clung to his back as he rode Jori Song's motorbike out into the country (although we weren't being shot at by the alternate-universe Evil Time Bureau). We've had very deep and meaningful conversations about life, and time, and responsibility (but we didn't always have to fit them into three minutes at the end of the episode).

It's like being undercover. I could be exposed at any moment but only if I mess up and say too much. It's a total thrill.

It even makes ITP feel useful. ITP stands for Integration Through Positivity. Or Isn't This Pointless. It depends who you ask. Pottery and group hugs, to Promote Our Individuality, Embrace Our Diversity, and Capitalize Meaningless Phrases In General, all presided over by the frizzy-haired ethnically-beaded fairtrade-coffee-drinking Mizz Cooper. Except that Mizz Cooper has gone on a yogic retreat in a tent somewhere where they make butter out of yaks for the whole term, leaving the hugs to be delivered by Mrs. Ashe from the Science department. Mrs. Ashe of the lumpy waist-height monoboob, and the glasses-on-a-sparkly-string. The closest she's ever got to Cooperesque touchy-feeliness before was probably when she bought an organic banana by accident. It's like being told what periods are by the Queen.

At least I have Fili in my group this year. Plus Dai's Henry and Peroxide Eric. I like the idea of getting to know them a bit better. And it's perfect for everyone getting to know Ed a bit better, too.

Ashe sticks exactly to Cooper's lesson plans from last term, so after half an hour's team-building a meditation space out of eggboxes and cellophane, we get to the Contribution. In other lessons, the Contribution is known as "that part where you actually have to write stuff down." This time, it's "Share a happy memory."

OUTS.

TAN.

DING.

We get ten minutes' writing time, then we have to read them out.

Brendan Wilson's definition of "happy" makes Ashe turn purple in the face and rip the paper out of his hand before he can get more than three sentences in. Peroxide Eric has written about how much he likes pink fluffy bunny rabbits, Honey's is about buying a handbag, and Fili has written HAPPINESS IS OVERRATED in eyeliner on her paper, and just holds it up instead of reading it out. I'm starting to feel daft for taking it seriously, but then it's my turn.

I feel happy when I think about my boyfriend, Ed, and how we met. He was here on one of the Goldfinch summer courses for a few weeks, for physiotherapy, because he had an accident on his motorbike and hurt his knee. And all the other people who were here having physiotherapy were old women, so we kind of got talking this one time when I found him on the Manor steps playing "Lola" on his acoustic guitar, and then he stayed on for a few extra weeks just to hang out and talk about music and poetry and bikes, even after his knee was totally better. And now he's back in a different boarding school in London, so I won't see him for ages. But if I play that song I can still remember him sitting there, and it always makes me happy.

I can feel my face pinking up as I read. Out of the corner of my eye I can see Fili's eyebrow rise, curious, amused. The second I stop speaking, I start to panic. The "Lola" thing just came to me at the last minute. I've pushed too far: It's all way too daft. But then Henry reads his, which is about watching Dai jogging round the lake at 6 A.M. when he thinks no one's watching, when there's still a layer of foggy cloud sitting on it. His voice is all warm when he speaks: He even gets a little flush in his cheeks, too.

Fili's still looking at me with that eyebrow quirked, that little smile tugging at the corner of her mouth. I suppose she and Simon are a bit above that sort of thing, but hey, if it's good enough for Henry Kim, I guess being sappy and ridiculous is OK.

I'm in love, after all. I'm supposed to be a bit dorky.

It works anyway. By the afternoon, it's filtered back to Dai, who hums the chorus of "Lola" at me all through History.

By the next day, Ludo's started asking me questions about which school Ed's at, and where it is in London.

Sometimes, my own brilliance can be a bit of a burden.

I'm lucky, though. Ludo's pretty distracted with sucking Peroxide Eric's face, Fili always seems to be hurrying off somewhere at the end of every lesson, and anyway Ed isn't the big event of the week. Wednesday is the first meeting of the Performing Arts Group, for the grand announcement of what the Wassail performance will be.

Dai grabs me at the end of French and marches me down to the Performing Arts block on the far side of Stables. I've been in and out of the music rooms that lead off the foyer before, helping Dad Man move a bunch of weird African drums and jingly bells around over the summer. But I've never done more than peer through the windows at the auditorium itself. Venables is already flailing around on the stage, wearing a floaty white shirt that's got too many buttons undone. (Hairy chest. I make a mental note to keep Ed unfuzzy.) He's got his usual swarm of girlies in attendance, Scheherezade and Honey and Leila, flicking their hair and pouting up at him. There's a sort of smog of perfume in the air. Underneath it, patchouli oil and cigarettes, from the Upper School arts geeks. And that strange dusty smell of velvet seats, like an ancient cinema.

"Come on in, guys, take a pew," Venables yells, waving his arms, and sending his if-I-keep-it-long-no-one-will-notice-I'm-going-bald hair flapping around his face. "Doesn't matter where you sit. Eat your lunch, pick your nose, do what you like, just need your attention thisaway. Brilliant. Love it. Brilliant."

Henry's already snagged us a row smack in the middle of the tiered seating, and he waves me and Dai over. Fili and Simon are there already, locked in their usual inaudible conversation.

The stinky patchouli people sit in the row in front of us. The Venablettes take up position at the very front, sitting up perkily straight. Everyone's conversations slowly get quieter and quieter, as if someone's leaning on the volume control.

"Where's . . ." I start to whisper.

There's a bang and a clatter from the doors. Ludo, breathlessly dragging a bored-looking Yuliya behind her.

"That's it, come in, come in," yells Venables, beckoning them in as they squeeze into the end of our row. "Plenty of room, folks. Brilliant. OK? OK. I think that's everyone. Let's get started, shall we?"

Total silence.

"Bloody hell, you guys are quiet! Can't have that. See lots of familiar faces here from last year, yeah? You guys know I don't do quiet. Theater doesn't do quiet. Theater needs you BIG and BRAVE, yeah?"

There's a mumble of "yeah"s in return.

"Can't hear you," says Venables, cupping his ear.

"Yeah."

"Still can't hear you! On your feet!"

The floor bounces slightly beneath my feet; everyone stands up. I look up at Timo Janusz's arse and realize I'm the only one not standing. Dai gives me a look till I give in.

"Let's get moving, come on! Hands in the air! Waggle them round! Pat your knees! Roll your shoulders back! Roll them forward! BIG and BRAVE, yeah?"

"Yeah!" yells everyone. Well, almost everyone. Fili is rolling her eyes as well as her shoulders. Yuliya is standing quite still, watching the whole thing with her mouth forming a perfect O of horror.

I decide I kind of like Yuliya.

"Heidi, come ON!" says Ludo over the chorus of yeah-ing, windmilling her arms. "You have to get into it properly!"

"Don't ever let me start a session without a warm-up, you guys, yeah?" bellows Venables, patting the air to tell us we can sit again. "Can't expect your brains to work if your bodies aren't moving, right?"

I usually expect my brain to work *instead* of my body moving, but Venables is blathering something about "kinetic energy" and rifling through his man-bag. Finally, he triumphantly thrusts a pale cream paperback book with old-fashioned black lettering on it toward us.

"Anyone recognize this?"

"It's a book," I say, automatically, and a teensy bit louder than planned.

"A book?" Venables cups his ear again. "Yes! It is! Never be afraid to state the obvious, guys. Nothing's obvious, yeah? But not just any book! It's a play, called *Twelfth Night*. Pretty famous. The guy that wrote it is pretty famous, too. The biggest celeb of the literary world? Shakespeare, guys!"

There's a vague murmuring around the auditorium.

"Come on, I know what you guys are all thinking. It tells us it's boring! Old Billy Shakespeare: words no one understands, nobody knows what's going on, everybody gets stabbed at the end, yeah?"

I have to give Venables a few points, there. We did *Hamlet* in English last year. I liked his proto-emo-kid thing, but I did write an entire essay about how it would've benefited from being forty-two minutes long, and finished with a paragraph that read, "In conclusion, NEEDS MORE JOKES." Prowse gave me a D.

People laugh anyway.

"Well, don't all rush for the doors yet, guys, yeah? Because first off, *Twelfth Night* is about cross-dressing and gay sex. And second of all, this play? Billy's play? That's not what we're doing."

He chucks the book over his shoulder. Someone claps.

"We're doing..." There's more rifling of the man-bag. "This!"

He unrolls a poster, with TWELFTH NIGHT: THE MUSICAL written in huge, crappy marker pen lettering.

HOE.

CAY.

Venables grins like a crazy monkey as mumbling starts up all over, and waves his arms a lot as he starts to tell everyone the plot. There are some impossibly identical boy-girl twins, and the girl dresses up like a boy, and a duke falls in love with him, which is apparently OK in Old Billy time because she's really a girl. Some guy wears comedy socks. And there's a clown.

"But forget all that stuff about dukes, guys. This is not 1601. No one is going to be wearing codpieces in this production. We're better than that, guys. We're going to set this somewhere crazy. Take our audience somewhere they didn't know they were going to go. Shake up our Shakespeare!"

Venables whips out a marker, and writes "IN THE '80s" on his poster, then adds "!!!!" on the end.

Fili makes a little moaning noise of despair.

"OH MY GOD!" hisses Ludo. "Leg warmers! And Lycra! And blue mascara!"

From the look on her face, these are apparently supposed to be good things.

Then we're all filtering back out of the comfy seats into the foyer to sign up for roles. The acting/singing people have to audition — not in front of everyone else — but I still wrestle the pen out of Dai's hand and cross my name off from where he's gleefully written it in. Detectives definitely stay backstage if there are going to be leg warmers involved. I hover over Set Design/Construction, but Timo and the patchouli gang are already signed up, and I'm not sure I can handle poetic angst while standing on a ladder. Simon's name is under Costume, though. I've never made anything more ambitious than my Bubble Wrap bag (and that's mostly held together with staples), but I always wanted to be one of those kitschy home-sewn kids. And Simon may need some assistance with colors that aren't black.

Costume it is.

The others are all on the audition pile, getting their stuff together to head back into the auditorium in little groups and sing songs from *Annie*, or whatever people do in auditions.

"Costumers? Brilliant, brilliant," Venables yells, flapping his arms and wafting me and Simon over to him. "Love it, yeah? Eighties. You know the eighties, yeah? Brilliant. Perfecto. And don't panic about construction, materials, budget, all that jazz. Right now, I just want your creativity. You can come up with some concept artwork for me, yeah? This time next week? Brilliant. Love it."

And then he flails off to be scarily enthusiastic in the direction of the props department.

"Can you draw?" I ask Simon, hopefully.

He shakes his head, blue-black hair dangling in his eyes.

"Know anything about the eighties?"

He shakes his head again, and picks a hole in his black nail varnish.

I feel a bit mean for thinking it, but Simon really is kind of weird. I mean, to the untrained eye, so is Fili, so I shouldn't judge. And my boyfriend's personal charms aren't necessarily all that obvious to anyone else, on account of me not having imagined them yet, so I'm not really in a position to snark. I suppose that's what love is: seeing the non-obvious best in someone.

Still, signing up for this job with uncommunicative Goth-boy was not the most stellar plan. Especially when I can't draw and also know nothing about the '80s, apart from what

I learned from TV. According to which the '80s were mostly very, very day-glo. In helicopters. And short shorts.

Probably not what Shakespeare had in mind, but it's a start.

My phone goes off inside my Bubble Wrap bag, sending the *Mycroft Christie Investigates* theme tune twanging out across the room. I burrow in my bag. The caller ID reads MOTHERSHIP.

I scrunch up my face, then scurry into the safety of Music Room 1 to answer.

"Babes? You're where? Oh. Right. You be good for Mr. Venables, now. What? Oh, yeah. Just wanted to remind you, I've got girls' aqua aerobics tonight, so you'll have to eat in the Dining Hall, babes, OK, and I'll pick you up after? Or if you'd rather wait, there's my things in the fridge, but don't have the blueberries, I'm going all blue tomorrow. Yes, I know traffic lights aren't blue. All right then, cheers, babes."

I perform a mental calculation involving the contents of my last pay envelope and the pizza delivery guy. The results are not good. Looks like Potatoes "R" Us for dinner again.

I shove the phone away and head for the foyer, knocking against a tub full of those spongy lollipop-shaped things you hit xylophones with and spilling a few.

"Twenty says she's dumped," I hear Dai say, as I stop to put them back.

HELL.

OH.

I hang back, for a little detecto-eavesdropping.

"You are SO mean! Ed totally wouldn't do that. Not on the phone anyway."

"He's in London, Ludo. What's he going to do, skywrite? I'm just saying, he can't be that into her. He hardly ever phones. He doesn't even text."

"Perhaps she's not that into him?" That's Henry. Hooray for Henry. I think.

"Henry! She is TOTALLY into him. Like, OBSESSO."

"She doesn't have a photo of him in her wallet." Dai again. No hooray for him.

"You looked?"

"Just out of curiosity. None on her ULife profile, either, which, by the way, still says she's single."

OOPS.

"Dai, sweetheart, I think you're the obsesso one."

"Henry, *sweetheart*, what's the background on your mobile phone?"

"A . . . picture of you and me."

"And Henry, *sweetheart*, how long have we been going out?"

"You may have a point."

"Maybe he's just too minging and gross for her to want to look at."

"OH MY GOD, Dai, he is SO not gross!"

"How would you even know?"

I decide that's probably enough, and do a big notice-me-coming cough as I come out from my Music Room 1 hiding place.

There's blushing and hair-tweaking and a general checking of watches, like the audition has already begun, and they're rehearsing Overplayed Pretending To Be Invisible. Apart from Yuliya, who has sat silent through the whole conversation as if it's very much beneath her (along with everything else), and Fili, who looks stony as always but is so, so amused on the inside. I think.

"Was that Ed on the phone, then?" says Dai, casual-like.

I nod.

"Everything OK?" says Ludo, looking hopeful on my behalf.

"He's . . . going through some stuff," I say, fiddling with my phone. "Having an identity crisis, kind of. It's a thing. No big. All fine. We're good."

Or we will be. Just as soon as I get my mental recipe book out again and start cooking.

Recipe for a Non-Imaginary Boyfriend

INGREDIENTS:

Frequent text messages o' love
Frequent phone calls o' love
Visibility in many photographs (preferably licking
  your face)
Presents
All the sexy sort of stuff
Actual existence in the real world

METHOD:

• Be in same room as nonfictional boyfriend.
• Attempt to resemble octopus.
• Repeat.

○ ○ ○ ○ ○ ○ ○ ○ ○ ○ ○ ○ ○ ○ ○ ○ ○ ○ ○ ○

I've been going about this all wrong. I get that now. I got all overexcited about the idea of me, snuggled up in Mycroft Christie's coat, listening to him — I mean *Ed* — talking about his heroic detective exploits, and forgot that it wasn't really me who needed to hear it. After all, it doesn't matter if I don't love Ed at all, so long as everyone else believes I do.

The gingerbread man on my desk looks despondent.

OK, he doesn't. But he looks like he might be thinking about it. I give him a reassuring little pat on the head.

I'm going to fix it anyway. I've constructed my pretty boy who falls off motorbikes and plays me songs on his guitar while tragically wounded. The basic recipe is awesome. Ed just needs to be a little more proactive, and a little less four inches high and leaning on my desk lamp.

The "actual existence" thing I'm skipping, obviously. And with Ed being off in London (somewhere) at his boarding school (which has no name), he can't be expected to participate in any octopus action. I don't need to handwrite cute Post-it notes to be left inside my copy of *Deutsch Heute*, like Dai keeps leaving for Henry. He's not required to sweep up behind me, wrap his hands over my eyes, and whisper filthy nothings into my ear, like Peroxide Eric. No sharing of mirror compact and the loan of dark cherry lipstick, like Simon does for Fili.

All of which I'm completely fine with. Especially the lipstick.

And thanks to the Mothership, I have the occasional phone call sewn up (so long as I can encourage her to ring me at random intervals, which will be easily achieved by me rearranging the fridge).

The rest, however, is a teensy bit more complicated.

I don't even know if you can text your own phone, but

caller ID will not be on my side, and my Little Leaf wages are not going to buy me a whole new phone. So texting is out.

The Little Leaf wages aren't going to run to deliveries of red roses and posh chocolates, either, and posting myself a bar of Cadbury Dairy Milk isn't going to have quite the same effect, so prezzies are out.

I can cut 'n' paste with the best of them, but a screencap of Mycroft Christie with my head Photoshopped onto Jori Song's is going to come out fugly. So the photo is out.

Which leaves . . . nothing.

And I've got to create a working scale model of the solar system out of drinking straws and bouncy balls, come up with those costume designs for PAG somehow, and write another Poem on an Autumn Leaf for Prowse.

It's impossible.

A dimly lit penthouse. Mycroft Christie, time-traveling gentleman detective, is admiring the view of the city of London. His delightful sidekick, Miss Heidi Ryder, is wearing pajamas with giraffes and looking sort of grumpy.

MYCROFT CHRISTIE: Nothing is impossible: only improbable.
HEIDI: Fancy seeing you here. And yeah, yeah, episode 2.1, "Ghost Town," explaining to Inspector Dedman that ghosts could've done all those murders, which you'd think he'd know what with him being one. This is supposed to help me how?

MYCROFT CHRISTIE: The solution may be closer to home than you realize, Inspector.

HEIDI: What's that supposed to mean? Ed is a ghost?

MYCROFT CHRISTIE: No, Heidi, Ed is not a ghost.

HEIDI: Eh?

MYCROFT CHRISTIE: I said, "No, Heidi, Ed is not a ghost."

HEIDI: But you don't say that. On the TV. In the show. You never say that.

MYCROFT CHRISTIE: I do now.

HEIDI: OK, I'm officially weirded out.

MYCROFT CHRISTIE: You're having an imaginary conversation with a character off the television. It took you until now to become "weirded out"?

HEIDI: Fair point. Actually, this is kind of cool.

MYCROFT CHRISTIE: Of course it is. That's why you're making it happen, you dork.

HEIDI: Mycroft Christie would never say "dork."

MYCROFT CHRISTIE: Madam, you can make me say whatever you like. Bum. Wee-wee. I'm leaving that hussy Jori Song behind, my darling, let's run away and detect things together!

HEIDI: Yes, please! Er, I mean, I couldn't possibly, I already have a boyfriend. And don't say "bum."

MYCROFT CHRISTIE: Make me.

HEIDI: OK. Done. You are now bottomless.

MYCROFT CHRISTIE: Very clever. Now, might we apply the same principle to young Edward?

HEIDI: Ed? I don't think I want him to be bottomless.

MYCROFT CHRISTIE: I was referring to your skills of ventriloquism. If you can make me say whatever you like, you can make Ed say whatever you like, too.

HEIDI: How does that help, if no one can hear it?

MYCROFT CHRISTIE: Your technology is rather unimpressive to a time traveler like myself, true enough, but I believe the internet might offer some assistance?

HEIDI: Ooh. *Ooh.* Actually, that could work.

MYCROFT CHRISTIE: Naturally.

HEIDI: But, if I made you say that, then I must've known it already, before you said it. So technically it must be my idea. Right?

MYCROFT CHRISTIE: (pouty face)

HEIDI: (sighs)

He's right, though. Or I am. You can be anyone you like on the internet. You can even be two people at once. I can log into my ULife whenever (and sneakily update my status to "in a relationship," just in case Dai happens to check again). But I can just as easily start a whole new ULife, with whatever name I choose, and it's like creating a whole new person for all the world to see.

I fire up the Dread Pirate Laptop, and get creative with my new ingredients. E-mail address, username, profile. I hesitate over the Profile Image option, wondering if Photoshopped Mycroft Christie really is the worst idea ever;

wondering if leaving it blank is just asking for suspicion. Then I catch the winking squished eye of my gingerbread man, and whip out my phone. One blurry camera phone upload later, and he's all set for public consumption.

The London penthouse. Miss Heidi Ryder is working hard at the desk, while Mycroft Christie, time-traveling gentleman detective, sulkily observes.

MYCROFT CHRISTIE: Edmund?

HEIDI: Only because edward.hartley@frogmail.com was already taken. I like it anyway. It sounds sophisticated.

MYCROFT CHRISTIE: Of course it does, my dear. And his disdain for television?

HEIDI: A cunning disguise so no one will guess he's me, mixed up with a few bits I borrowed off you.

MYCROFT CHRISTIE: Cunning indeed. Although your memory seems to be faltering: I believe, if you refer to episode 1.7, "Librarians Do the Funniest Things," you'll discover that my favorite book is *The Tell-Tale Times-ink*, by H. R. Pendellikon.

HEIDI: Shush. I am busy with my other imaginary boyfriend, whose interests are not allowed to be as made-up as yours.

I had to do quite a lot of Googling. But he seems like the kind of boy who might sit on the Manor steps and play songs to passing girls, the kind of boy the girls might stop and chat to, because of his effortless charm and good looks and knowledge of hipster writers I haven't read. Not the kind of boy who stops and talks to girls like *me*, anywhere but inside my crazy head. But that doesn't matter. They don't matter. I can make this Ed like me: That's all that counts.

He still needs to talk, though.

I click on "Post to ULife," and hover my hands over the keyboard.

Subject: first post

Good evening.

Too formal.

Hey you guys!

Too Venables-esque.

hey

It's a typo, but I like it. It's his typing schtick: He's lower-case ed, too cool for the shift key. I can even go back and edit "e. e. cummings" into his "Likes" list, just for consistency.

heidi made me come on this site so i can talk to her because apparently i never do

OK, way to cast yourself as Whiny Girlfriend #1.

heidicakes has an account here so i just had to as well so i could tell her how gorgeous she is!!!

Ick. He's imaginary, not blind and delusional. And "Heidicakes"?

so i guess i should update this or something, since it's here, and i'm feeling kind of lonely.

This, I like. He's melancholy, nonchalant, and all those other things people only are in poems.

i guess h is the only one who'll read it anyway.

I like the "h" thing. No one's ever called me "h" before.

sorry for not phoning much this week, bb, got caught texting in media studies and mr smith has confiscated my phone.

My boyfriend, last of the great rebels. (And Mr. *Smith*? Come on, brain.)

sorry i haven't been calling much. been trying to get the bike running again, marco's got me some shifts at the garage, still doing physio. plus whenever i have to hang up it just reminds me how far away you are.

Yeah, baby. He's probably crying a Single Perfect Tear through the grease marks on his face as he sweats over his big foxy motorbike.
Too much?
Well, yes, but I don't care.

you'll only yell at me for trying to get back on the bike anyway, amirite? :P

Does Ed say :P?

you'll only yell at me for trying to get back on the bike anyway, right?

OK, he's going to have to say :P, otherwise it looks like we're having an argument, and it's a bit too soon in our relationship for us to be fighting.

how's tricks? am bored out of my mind already. new roommate guy continues to suffer personal hygiene issues.

Too prissy for manly motorbike boyfriend.

new roommate bilbo continues to smell. mostly of socks. think he has just the one pair. suggestions?

I start formulating cute banter immediately. Brilliant. We really are an adorable couple.

ok, getting dragged out of the door for a run. would bring laptop with me and keep typing, but i'm not quite that talented. (ok, i am exactly that talented, i just don't want to dazzle you from afar, it's too cruel.) thanks for the parcel. marco says "hello heidi like your picture nice to know he didn't just invent you to make his summer sound less crappy."

i have to go now so i can hit him on your behalf.

ok, really going now. miss you like tuesday afternoons,

ed

The penthouse. Mycroft Christie, time-traveling gentle-man detective, leans over Miss Heidi Ryder's elegant shoulder to assess her work.

MYCROFT CHRISTIE: A commendable effort, young lady. The validation of your story from the mythical "Marco" is particularly astute.

HEIDI: Why, thank you. I like the way I've sent him an invisible present: I'm totally doing that again with everyone at Christmas.

MYCROFT CHRISTIE: I wish you luck. Might I inquire as to the significance of Tuesday afternoons?

HEIDI: Picnics under the cherry tree by the lake. I figure the "miss you like . . ." thing can be a running gag between us. You know, every time he posts he says something from our many happy hours together: I miss you like sharing apple pie, I miss you like holding hands in the sunset . . .

MYCROFT CHRISTIE: I miss you like correct speech and punctuation?

HEIDI: Shut it, future boy. You've got a malfunctioning Twenty-First-Century Linguistic Etiquette Implant, which makes you talk like a loon. Ed doesn't.

MYCROFT CHRISTIE: I'm not sure this young man is a good influence on you. You're getting rather cheeky.

HEIDI: Who, me? (fluttery eyelashes)

MYCROFT CHRISTIE: (smoldery eyebrow, jealous look)

HEIDI: Ahem. Yes. Do you think I should add some kisses at the end?

MYCROFT CHRISTIE: As you'll recall from the undelivered letter in episode 2.12, "The Charge D'Affaire Affair," my preferred sign-off is "With love & affection."

HEIDI: It's a good job you're pretty, isn't it?

MYCROFT CHRISTIE: (sighs, continues smoldery eyebrow to fade-out)

And that's it. He's done. Gingerbread Ed Hartley, fresh from the oven, and ready to serve.

ORES.

UM.

I'm kind of desperate to show him off right away, but I have to be a professional about this. My many hours of TV detective training have taught me the importance of patience: of hanging back and waiting for the quarry to take the bait, in case the quarry turns out to be flying manmonkeys of death. Not that I'm exactly expecting that. And Mycroft and Jori on stakeout eating doughnuts definitely get to have more fun than I do sitting in History, trying to casually steer a conversation about Henry VIII round to hot boyfriendly types. But blurting out, "Please go and look at this website where you will find convincing evidence of how much Ed loves me," could ruin the whole operation.

Result: I'm practically skipping when I hit the Little Leaf for my next shift and get to at least share Ed with *someone*.

I dutifully strap on my frilly apron, and admire today's Wisdom: OUR BLUE POPPY SEED CAKE IS NOT ACTUALLY BLUE: JUST THE POPPY SEEDS IN IT. SORRY TO DISAPPOINT. I sling the usual toast, jam, English Breakfast pot for two at the ancient couple seated at the window. I wait for Betsy to get us set up with our own pot. Then I whack the Dread Pirate onto the counter, piggyback onto the Big Bean's wi-fi network from across the road, and introduce Betsy to gingerbread_ed in all his ULife glory.

I don't even dare hold my cup while she's reading. She's going to love him. She's going to think he's heaven on a stick.

She makes the face she makes when people ask for their tea with lemon. It's not a happy face.

"Oh, *Heidi*. It's sweet and all, but don't you think this is a little too much?"

PARD.

ON.

MOY?

"You don't think he sounds yummy? In an angsty troubadour kind of way?"

Betsy sighs, and casts her eye over the screen again.

"I guess, if you like that intense thing. He's like an independent movie Ken doll. One of those guys who wants to read you his poetry while wearing a Che Guevara T-shirt."

"That's bad?"

I could be read poetry. I've already been read poetry. By the lake, all summer, under the cherry tree. I've just decided. I've always pictured him in a sort of geek-chic flowery shirt before now, but Ed could totally rock a Che T-shirt. In a post-political post-ironic don't-really-know-what-this-means kind of way.

"It's bad if the poetry is bad, hon. Which, let's face it, it's going to be. Have you ever actually read Jack Kerouac?"

"No. But Ed would love it. It's required reading for open-roading big-sky biker types. Like how all emogirls have to read *The Bell Jar*."

"Uh-huh."

Betsy takes a long sip of tea.

"Oh My God. You don't like my boyfriend."

Betsy squints from under her hair. "No, no, no, honeybee. He's . . . cute as a button. And you're obviously enjoying yourself, making all this up. It's just he's, I don't know, maybe a little more revealing than you realize? He's not a person, after all: He's a list of things Heidi finds attractive in a guy. That's kind of personal material to be putting out there, hon. It's like I'm peeking inside your head, getting all surprised by what's going on up there."

"Surprised?" That doesn't sound good. I thought Ed was perfect and gorgeous in a universally accepted, non-Heidi-specific kind of way. "You mean, I got the list of attractive stuff wrong?"

"No, sweetie. That's not the kind of thing you can get

wrong. I guess . . . well, I guess I'm just surprised you *have* a list."

"Don't let The Coat fool you, missy," I say, waving a spoon at her. "Beneath this cunning disguise, I am actually a girl. A girly girl, who has girly thoughts about boylike boys. Bad thoughts. Bad, naughty, girly thoughts."

There's a little cough, cutting me off from my spoon waving.

Teddy.

Edging behind Betsy and looking deliriously rumpled like always, curls askew, in a floury apron and his monster-feet slippers.

I don't know what's more humiliating: the fact that he heard me, or the fact that he's giving me that sympathetic lazy smile, eyes twinkling, the one that says, "Wow, you're probably really embarrassed now."

I sort of shrink into The Coat, waiting for him to swat me mockingly with a spoonful of cookie dough, or doodle a chalky motorbiking Heidi-lover (wearing very thick spectacles). But he just twinkles knowingly some more, and turns his back.

"I'll just be over here, completely unable to hear you," he says, gently enough to make me shrink even farther, while he gets busy wiping down the Daily Wisdom and replacing it with WHY NOT TRY A CUP OF EARL GREY? *WE HAVE RUN OUT OF MILK.* "Again?" says Betsy, twisting round to read. "Crap. Teddy, sweetie, drop round the corner store and pick up a couple of pints? Excuse me, Heidi, I have to go yell at some suppliers."

We've only got two customers, and they've been served. We're milkless. Perfect opportunity for me to do what any self-respecting girlfriend would be doing right now: chat online with my boy.

UChat

mrsheidichristie: Hey eddiebaby! You still alive or did Bilbo stink you to death?

gingerbread_ed: he stank me to death. apparently i have been reincarnated as some guy called 'eddiebaby.' :/

mrsheidichristie: Humblest apologies, edmondo.

gingerbread_ed: aren't you supposed to be at work?

mrsheidichristie: Yeah, we're not very busy though. Betsy says hi!

gingerbread_ed: give her a snog from me?

mrsheidichristie: um . . . no. I could send you an almond finger?

gingerbread_ed: mmm, kinky

I have to switch between two different browsers so I can be logged into both accounts, which is a pain. But it's worth it. It looks super-amazing. Even Betsy's impressed, when she comes back in.

"OK, I'm starting to like him," she says, reading over my shoulder once I'm safely logged back out again, my tracks covered. "You, I'm a little worried about. You're a little too good at this, you know that?"

"It's all Ed's fault. He's leading me astray."

She smiles. I think she's finally getting why this is fun. Then she peers at the screen again.

"Wait. These are private messages, right? So only you and Ed can read them? I mean, in theory."

See? She's starting to think he's real, too.

"In theory, yeah."

"So if no one else can see this stuff, what's the point?"

I check my watch, and grin.

Mycroft Christie, episode 2.2, "The Burmese Falcon." *Contrary to popular belief, my dear, I know precisely what I'm doing.*

The Little Leaf door opens with a jingle, and in walks my audience.

The Leftover Squad. Full lineup: Ludo, snuggled halfway inside Peroxide Eric's military coat; Fili and Simon, the doom twins, gauntly perfect in identical black skinnies and pointy boots; Dai, bouncing in like Tigger and propelling Henry forward to show him off.

Betsy raises an eyebrow.

"Hey, guys, was wondering if you'd make it," I say, ultra-casual, gently nudging the Dread Pirate to ensure the screen is enticingly visible.

I catch Betsy's eye.

OWE.

YES.

Phase Two of Operation: Authentic Boy is going perfectly to plan.

The Lovely Safak drops in to see Teddy, and helps out in

74

the kitchen between kissy-breaks. I scribble down orders, smirking as Simon requests the most Goth items on the menu (black currant tea and Darkest Chocolate Brownies) for them both, without Fili having to say a word. I worry for a minute at Henry's amused look, as he takes in the mismatched mugs and the worn bit on the arm of the sofa: He's probably used to posh china and waitresses who don't spill things on you. But Betsy threatens to force-feed Dai cream teas if he gets anymore buff (which makes him go all pink, even though you can tell he's loving it), and Henry shakes her hand and they geek out together over Ceylon versus Darjeeling. Peroxide Eric sprawls on the green velvet sofa, Ludo snuggling pointedly farther into his coat, one beady eye enviously watching Safak lean over the counter to ruffle the flour out of Teddy's hair.

And I observe, invisibly, as Dai's curiosity drags him to sneak a peek at the open laptop; as he whispers gleefully to Ludo, who then quite urgently needs a teaspoon and to linger at the counter, reading, while she's finding one; as the laptop catches Fili's eye too while she's waiting in the bathroom queue and she blinks at it; while Dai and Ludo watch and giggle from the sofa.

"So, what's up?" I say innocently, hopping up on the nearest table.

Ludo, Dai, and Henry exchange smirky and faintly guilty looks.

"Dai's being a crazy dumb person," says Ludo, barely missing a beat.

This is even better than I'd hoped. Now they're pretending Ed is their little secret, too.

"Afraid so," says Henry, smoothly picking up the thread like a pro. "Mr. Busy and Important here has decided he's too good for slumming it on the stage."

"Even though it's going to be, like, THE thing that everyone is doing, and we're, like, never even going to SEE him this term if he doesn't," adds Ludo.

Dai throws up his hands. "All I said was I might not be able to do swimming *and* squash club *and* the musical. Which is apparently the end of the world."

"He thinks he did a bad audition," explains Henry, fondly.

"Not true," says Fili.

"And Fili would know," Henry adds. "Secret starlet, this one. Everyone else is wailing about vocal warm-ups and 'what's my motivation,' and she just stands up and sings. No accompaniment. Note-perfect, clear as a bell. Best audition I've ever heard."

"Really?" says Peroxide Eric, shifting around on the sofa, and sliding his eyes up and down Fili thoughtfully. "Now that's what I call a hidden talent."

Ludo gives him a prod with a glossy peach fingernail, but I don't think he means it in a sarky way. Fili doesn't seem to, either. I mean, she rolls her eyes, but there's definitely a little smile at the corners of her lips.

I try to imagine '80s-styled glittery musical superstar Fili. It's . . . weird.

"Anyway, Phil hasn't even DECIDED on the casting yet, so he should totally just wait."

"You're calling him *Phil* now?" says Peroxide Eric.

"You wouldn't understand, baby, but calling him Mr. Venables is, like, SO not an accurate representation of the director/cast dynamic?"

Ludo rubs Peroxide Eric's chest reassuringly. He gives her a little pat on the head, and throws me a pleading look.

"You'll help me restrain her, Heidi, right? Before I lose her to the theater geeks forever?"

I nod, and grin. I'm starting to like Peroxide Eric.

Betsy strides up to collect a few mugs.

"Hope all these adorable couples aren't making you feel lonesome, honeypie," she says, leaning on my shoulder. "You with the long-distance relationship and all, I mean."

She gives me a huge wink. My heart does a little fandango of panic. This was not part of the plan. Phase Two is at a crucial stage: a crucial, fundamental, going-to-be-really-hard-to-explain-away-as-a-joke-now stage. One wrong move, and it could be Frog Girl time forever.

Dai and Ludo are both sitting perkily upright now, like two meerkats. Henry and Peroxide Eric look sweetly intrigued. Simon and Fili have their heads bent, doing their mumblespeaking thing.

"Of course!" says Dai. "The Divine Betsy has actually *met* the Mysterious Ed."

I have no idea what my face is doing, but my throat

feels like someone inserted marshmallows. Many, many marshmallows.

Betsy slaps on an even bigger grin, and tugs on one of my braids.

"I don't know about Mysterious. Lickable, maybe? Nope: *edible*, that's the word. And Dai, sweetie, I couldn't get those two off of that sofa all summer. Could've stopped putting sugar out on the tables, they sweetened up the place all by themselves."

Then she plumps a kiss on the side of my head, and disappears off toward the kitchen, muttering something improbable about having heard the oven timer go "ping."

Everyone is looking my way.

I prepare to explain away Gingerbread Ed's blatant fictionalness. With . . . words. Words that I will think of. Soon. Really soon.

"*Edible*," sighs Ludo, into Peroxide Eric's chest.

"Betsy seal of approval," says Fili slowly, her eyes flicking between the kitchen and me, suddenly looking a whole lot more interested.

"Get you, Slutgirl," says Dai. "Not that we would've expected any less. I always figured you'd be the picky type."

"Dai, I think you're embarrassing her," says Henry.

"She's remembering what she got up to on this sofa," says Dai. "The Sofa of Sex."

Ludo squeals, and claps her hands.

Even Peroxide Eric looks quietly impressed.

OHM.

EYE.

GOD.

Phase Two is apparently kind of successful. Like, a lot. Like, way more than I even hoped.

Mycroft Christie's going to dance me around the penthouse in celebration tonight, I can tell. And then Ed will probably send me a few more messages, telling me how amazing I am, and I'll send a few to him, and not even the Mothership announcing another Green Only week can possibly bring me down.

The rest of the day goes by like a blur. I'm actually confused when Betsy starts the closing up routine of mopping, wiping, and eating leftover cake. I guess that's what happens when you're in love.

"Earth calling Heidi," says Betsy, knocking on my forehead and handing me a weary-looking scone. "We interrupt this transmission to tell you to go home, in the nicest possible way."

"Sorry. I was just . . ."

"About to say, 'Thank you, Betsy, for your Oscar-worthy performance today'?"

I grin. She was kind of awesome.

"Thanks. If they need an understudy for the musical, I'll know who to call."

"Yeah, heard you guys talking about it. You need any time off for rehearsals and such, hon, that's OK."

"Oh, I'm not acting. Me and Fili's boyfriend are supposed to be doing costume designs. Which is kind of . . . unhappenable."

Betsy is familiar with my artistic non-skills. Even my stick men could do with improvement.

"Well, if it's sketches you need, just ask the resident artist."

She nods toward the back wall, where today's batch of Teddy's cheery chalky doodlemen are dancing their way across the list of specials.

I wrinkle my nose without really meaning to.

"Um. Yeah. That's really kind, but . . ."

"You don't want my boy's crappy scribbles all over your fancy schoolwork?"

That is sort of what I mean, though I hope my face doesn't show it. That kind of thing is cute on the wall of the Little Leaf: I'm not sure they'll really fly up on the hill.

She chuckles. "Hey, Teddy! Get your head out of the oven and get out here! He's actually pretty good, you know. As in, 'applying to art school' kind of good?"

"Ignore the Proud Mommy routine, please?" he says, giving me one of his easy, lazy smiles. The kind that makes me do a little Homer Simpson drooly thing inside my head. The kind that Ed *totally* gets jealous about.

"Art school, huh?" I manage to say. "Wow. That's great. I didn't even know there were any around here."

"Won't be around here — if I get in. I'll have to do some classes for credit first, but I'm looking at a few places out East: maybe Chicago?"

"Whoa. That's . . . you'll be . . . a long way away. I mean, um, who's going to make Teddy's Toffee Temptation cake?"

It's not exactly what I mean. I might miss more than the cake.

But Teddy's tilting his head anyway, the smile turning awkward. Betsy twists her daisy rings, and looks at me furtively through her hair.

"Nothing's set, OK, hon? That's why I didn't want to say anything yet. But I guess you're entitled to know. I'm selling the Little Leaf. Maybe." She takes hold of my hand and squishes it between both of hers, though hers seem to be the ones that are shaky. "You might've noticed, we're not exactly blessed with a million customers lately. You wouldn't think it, but summer was slow this year. We're kind of going under, honeypie. And Teddy's dad says he'll pay for Teddy to go to school if it's over there, so, you know. The timing's not so bad, really. Sometimes you've just got to read the signs, go with flow, land wherever the wind wants to blow you."

I don't know what to say.

Well, I do. *Don't go. Don't leave me here. Don't spoil my perfect day. Stay here forever and ever with your cake and your tea and your unattainably picturesque Teddy, and your being the one person I can tell anything.*

"How long?" I mumble, instead.

"If it happens, we'll probably aim to be back over there for Christmas." Betsy frowns as she sees my face go all crumply. "But we'll keep you on for as long as we can, honey, I promise. And you'll always be welcome."

"I'll do those pictures for your school thing, too," says Teddy, shuffling his feet. "Whatever you need. You can drop in any time to talk it over. Doesn't need to be a Saturday. You know, weekday, evening, whenever you like?"

He's trying so hard to be nice. It makes it worse, somehow.

Betsy packs my scone in a paper bag, wraps me up in The Coat, and gives me a hug in the doorway before she locks up.

The bell jingles behind me, like there's something to be cheerful about.

All I want to do is hide in my room and watch *Mycroft Christie Investigates*: a really wallowy miserable one like episode 2.11, "Through the Looking Glass," so I can have a sad cry about Jori Song's tragic childhood, and not have to contemplate my own. (Or at least hope that mine turns me into an ass-kicking sidekicky type with only moderate daddy issues.)

But the Mothership has made Red Pepper and Tomato soup, and apparently I have to help her eat it.

"You'll find another job, babes," says the Mothership. "Bet that coffee place across the road will be hiring. It's always heaving in there!"

UM.

THANKS?

"I don't want to work in the Big Bean coffee shop. And it's not the job I'm upset about."

The Mothership puts on her Kind Teacher Listening face.

"I know it's a bit awkward for you, babes, not having as much money to throw around as the other kids at school. And it's nice that you care so much. But don't get yourself in a knot about it. Maybe it's for the best? Mr. Prowse keeps mentioning you to me in the staff room — and not in the nice way, babes. You don't need too many distractions this year. And it is only a café closing down. It's not the end of the world."

I think that's half the problem. I'm quite familiar with apocalypses: If we only have twelve hours before the fabric of time collapses in on itself and sucks us into a singularity, I've got a plan all worked out. I can cope fine with the world ending: It's the world being unfair I can't manage.

After dinner, I stomp up to the attic, and lie on my bed. My gingerbread boy is still there, leaning nonchalantly against my desk lamp, his buttons looking especially shiny.

He's a rubbish boyfriend, Gingerbread Ed. If I were Ludo, Peroxide Eric would be sweeping me into his arms, wrapping his coat around me in a big wool-scratchy hug, and snogging all my woes away. If I were Dai, Henry would be doing something ultra-practical and dynamic, like promising to phone his dad to ask him to buy the Little Leaf, just to cheer me up. If I were Fili, Simon would be expressing his deep concern by, well, probably just holding my hand and looking a bit miserable. But at least he'd be there.

Mycroft Christie would explode something on my behalf, and then look attractively guilty while pretending he did it for The Greater Good of Humanity or whatever.

We all simply want to belong.

That's still what I want: to belong, to fit in, to know I'm not ever going to feel like a lonely Frog Girl again. Only I think maybe there are different kinds of loneliness, different kinds of belonging. Maybe I don't just want to belong to a somewhere. Maybe I want to belong with a *someone*: a real one, the kind who isn't made of crumbs and ground ginger.

But I suppose, sometimes, a girl just has to take care of herself.

I whack the Dread Pirate on the desk and drum my fingers, plotting. Ed's probably worried about his Heidi. We probably had a very moving conversation earlier on the phone. He's probably writing a song about me right now, strumming his guitar, wishing he were here. . . .

I log into Ed's account, and wiggle my fingers over the keyboard.

A text box flashes up before I've even given Ed a subject line.

UChat

ludovica_b: Hi Ed!!!!!!!!!!!!!!!!!!
ludovica_b: Just wanting to say Hi!!!!!
ludovica_b: We are all excited to meet you. :)

WOE.

UH.

It's Ludo. Ludo, talking to Ed. Ludo, talking to Ed, like Ed is real. Suddenly, me hanging out with Mycroft Christie doesn't seem quite so bonkers.

Guess Ed had better reply, then?

gingerbread_ed: hey ludo

ludovica_b: OMG you are there!

ludovica_b: Hiiiiiiiii

ludovica_b: I'm Heidi's friend btw

gingerbread_ed: i know

gingerbread_ed: i mean, she told me about you

ludovica_b: OMG!!!!

gingerbread_ed: feels like i know you already

ludovica_b: haha!

ludovica_b: why are you gingerbread?

gingerbread_ed: long story

gingerbread_ed: ask heidi :)

ludovica_b: got to go bb

gingerbread_ed: say hi to eric from me

ludovica_b: OMG you know EVERYTHING!!!

gingerbread_ed: i do my best

I feel kind of giddy. And brilliant. And sick. And urgently in need of some explanation of the gingerbread thing.

Ed bought it for me as a parting gift. Got Betsy to make a special one that I could keep forever: presented it to me in the Little Leaf, while we were snuggled up on the Sofa of Sex. The squishy eye is intentional. He's giving me a flirty little wink, just to make sure I don't forget him — as if I could . . .

I'm getting a bit too good at this, I think. And then the screen winks at me again, and I see a little envelope appear at the top of Ed's page.

Message from: dai_fawr <dafydd.wyndavies@goldfinch.ac.uk>
Hey dude,

OK, so she says she didn't, but I know she messaged you — so in case you were wondering, Ludo is not actually a psycho stalker. She just comes off like that sometimes. Just in case you were thinking you were being harassed by nutters.

Don't run away screaming from Ryder because her friends resemble the clinically insane, right? Cos I think she really likes you.

Later dude,
Dai (also not a psycho stalker)

The giddy feeling comes back. I know you're not supposed to want your friends to talk about you behind your back. But this is different. This is them, up on the hill, talking about me, and Ed, and how Ludo is insane, and it's giving me warm fuzzies all over.

Cos I think she really likes you, says Dai.

AW.

Message from: gingerbread_ed <gingerbread_ed@frogmail.com>

hey dai the notstalker,

she came off more as someone who'd fallen asleep on the ! key than the clinically insane. but thanks for the reassurance. do you do this for all your friends' boyfriends?

h likes me? that's lucky. i kinda like her too.

ed

Message from: dai_fawr <dafydd.wyndavies@goldfinch.ac.uk>

Hey dude,

No, I don't do this for all my friends. I just know Ludo. Don't tell Ryder I said this, but Ludo has a tendency to go chasing after blokes. Other people's blokes. Well, any blokes, really. Not stirring: just a heads up.

Later dude,
Dai, Still Not A Stalker (think my bloke would be unimpressed by that as a career move)

Message from: gingerbread_ed <gingerbread_ed@frogmail.com>

hey dai,

ta for the info.

tell your henry he's got nothing to worry about: i am definitely not your type. though h says he's very cute, maybe i should worry about her chasing other people's blokes instead . . . :)

ed

I hit REFRESH a few more times, wondering if Dai's got any more cutely attentive advice for my boy on how to escape Ludo's clutches (ha!), or if Fili's going to join in the meet-and-greet. I'd love her to meet Ed. I bet they'd get on brilliantly, once they got over that awkward stuttery phase at the beginning and started really talking. I bet they'd be like old friends in no time at all. But I suppose she's busy with her beloved boy. Just like me.

The penthouse. Mycroft Christie, debonair detective, is performing the tango with his glamorous (yet intellectual) companion, Miss Heidi Ryder.

MYCROFT CHRISTIE: You seem rather pleased with yourself, my dear.

HEIDI: I made a whole person, and I'm pretty sure Mr. Klee told us in Biology that it usually takes about nine months. So, yeah. Go me!

MYCROFT CHRISTIE: Indeed. Very well done.

HEIDI: Do you have to be quite that patronizing?

MYCROFT CHRISTIE: I'm afraid it's in the script. It encourages you to be feisty and sarcastic in return, in order for us to reveal our unresolved sexual tension through snarky banter.

HEIDI: Oh, yeah. I have a boyfriend now, though.

MYCROFT CHRISTIE: According to season 3, I have a secret wife from the future who's been sent back through time to kill me. I think we must accept, my dear, that our romance is somewhat star-crossed.

HEIDI: Good point. I hope Ed doesn't turn out to have a secret wife from the future. Yours was rubbish.

MYCROFT CHRISTIE: I'm not sure I approve of this emboldened Miss Ryder. You're terribly spirited.

HEIDI: My boyfriend's made from gingerbread: I still have plenty of unresolved sexual tension to go around. Now do us both a favor, Mr. Christie, and shut up.

Miss Heidi Ryder plucks a rose stem from a vase, thrusts it between Mycroft Christie's teeth, and begins to lead the dance.

Recipe for *Twelfth Night* by William Shakespeare

INGREDIENTS:

Identical girl/boy twins (Viola and Sebastian)
Lovestruck Duke Orsino
Olivia, the posh bird he fancies
Malvolio, an annoying butler
Feste, the world's most depressing clown
Sword-fighting comedy lords
Drunk people
Confusing gay subtext
A big boat

METHOD:

• Crash big boat on an island, causing Viola (the girl twin) and Sebastian (the boy twin) to become separated and think the other is dead.
• Lightly whisk Viola until she decides to dress up like a boy called Cesario.
• Add Olivia, who falls in love with Cesario (who is a girl).

• Add Orsino, who also falls in love with Cesario (which isn't technically a gay fling as he is a girl, but then Orsino doesn't know that).

• Mix remaining lords, drunks, servants, and clowns into a big gloppy mess.

• At last minute, throw Sebastian into the bowl.

• Finish with some convenient marriages between Not Gay At All Orsino and his very female bride Viola, and Not Gay At All Olivia and her conveniently identical-to-his-sister husband Sebastian.

• Perform repeatedly for 400 years.

Recipe for *Twelfth Night: The Musical!* by Phil Venables, with help from Mr. W. S.

INGREDIENTS:

Identical girl/boy twins (Viola and Sebastian)
Lovestruck niteclub manager Duke
Olivia, the rival bar owner he fancies
Malcolm Malvolio, pop impresario
Feste, a barfly

Stiletto-wielding podium dancers

Drunk people

Confusing gay subtext

A spaceship

METHOD:

• Crash spaceship into planet Earth in 1983, causing space travelers from Mars Viola (the girl twin) and Sebastian (the boy twin) to become separated and think the other is dead.

• Repeat above method, substituting ingredients as appropriate, while listening to "Tainted Love" by Soft Cell.

• Perform once, hopefully, at the end-of-term Wassail party.

○ ○ ○ ○ ○ ○ ○ ○ ○ ○ ○ ○ ○ ○ ○ ○ ○ ○ ○ ○

I hit the Dining Hall with my head full of pre-prepared answers to Ed questions and glum thoughts about the Little Leaf, but my love life and the impending departure of cake, wages, and nice non-Finchy people have to take a backseat. The *Twelfth Night: The Musical!* cast list is out.

"It's just TOTALLY unfair. I mean, there should be RULES or something." Ludo rests her chin on Peroxide Eric's big padded shoulder. "Don't you think there should be RULES or something?"

I expect Ed has comfy shoulders, for me to cutely perch my chin on.

Peroxide Eric yawns, and shrugs. "I don't get the big badness. You all have parts, right? Speaking roles, singing, all of that?"

He's right. Henry is going to be Duke, the main guy. Fili is Feste, the sad clown, which is somehow the most perfect thing in the world. Ludo is Maria the niteclub cleaner: not the biggest role in the world, but she has lots of scenes with Malcolm Malvolio — and that's Dai.

"Except for those of us who didn't actually want to run around on stage wearing tinfoil, right, Heidi?" Peroxide Eric adds, giving me a wink.

"And Simon," murmurs Fili.

Simon raises his hand, like we're in assembly.

"It's not about who's not in it," says Dai, slumping over a plate of floppy salad. "It's about who *is*."

"It's all right for you," says Henry, nudging him. "I'm the one who's got to pretend to fall in love with her."

Peroxide Eric looks blank.

"Scheherezade Adams," supplies Fili.

"Scheh . . . she's the one with the . . . ?"

"Nose job," says Ludo firmly, before Eric can actually perform his very ill-advised mime. "And HELLO SURPRISE, she's Viola. Like, the main girl. The heroine. The best part? When she, like, TOTALLY can't even sing or anything. She just points her boobage at people and they're, like, deaf and blind or something."

"On the upside, she has to dress up like a boy for most of the play," I say. "The boobage will be under wraps. Squished. They'll probably have to tape them down."

Silence.

"What?"

Henry pats me gently on the arm. "I believe we're admiring your enthusiasm."

"Hey, I think Heidi could be on to something," says Peroxide Eric, tugging on the dangly part of the piercing in his lip and grinning. "If the source of all her evil power is boobage, maybe she's like Samson, you know? Tape down the bazoinkas and she's just an ordinary tone-deaf mortal."

"Did you just say *bazoinkas*?" says Ludo, jabbing him with a finger.

"I'm still stuck on *boobage*," murmurs Simon. "Not literally," he adds, taking Fili's hand.

Dai sighs. "You get to be followed around by a lovesick model, too, Henry. It's every cliché you've ever dreamed of."

Yuliya has somehow landed the role of Olivia, despite it presumably involving opening her mouth and sounds coming out.

"We could rehearse together!" says Ludo, her Yuliya fangirling undimmed by lack of actual conversation. "I could totally come up to your room, Fili, and we could, like, practice, all three of us together!"

Fili doesn't reply. Which isn't all that unusual, really, but somehow Detective Heidi suspects she's not replying in a way that means "no."

Even Ludo notices.

"Well, not yet, obviously, because we haven't had the scripts yet," she says, doubtfully, tucking her hair behind one ear.

Fili goes on not replying.

It's weird. I mean, Ludo's idea of rehearsal with Fili and Yuliya is going to involve a lot of wanting to try on all of Yuliya's clothes and not a whole lot of rehearsing, obviously. But Fili would just roll her eyes, and give Ludo a serious dose of eyebrowing till she shuts up. At least, that's how it used to be.

I start thinking about how I've been waiting for the Mothership on the balance beam alone: all the non-conversations I haven't been having with Fili this term. If she's fallen out with Ludo for some reason, I haven't had much chance to find out why.

Henry gives Dai a tap on the back, rescuing the conversation. "Try not to panic, darling. If the worst comes to the worst, I can always try acting. I hear it's very popular in musical theatre."

Dai shrugs, and goes on poking at his salad. Detective Heidi notices something weird there, too, though I'm not sure what. Dai can't really be jealous of Scheherezade and Yuliya, for obvious Very Gay Indeed reasons. But something's not right.

"Are you really going to make us wear tinfoil, Heidi?" says Ludo.

I glance at Simon, my companion in costuming. Well, in theory. He blinks back at me through his hair, and shrugs.

"We haven't really figured out the specifics yet," I say, feeling mildly panicky. "Actually, I've kind of got something else on my mind at the moment. Not really a school thing, but . . . well, I kind of had some bad news. About the Little Leaf?"

There's a horrible squawk, as Dai scrapes his chair back from the table.

"Sorry. Got to hit the pool."

"Don't mind him, he hasn't had his vitamins today," Henry throws over his shoulder, hurrying out after him.

I look around, hoping someone else is going to ask if I'm OK, but Ludo and Peroxide Eric are a bit preoccupied with a random brunch-table snog. I look to Fili, hoping she'll rescue me, or at least exchange a quick eyeroll, but she's watching them with an odd look on her face.

"Homework," she says quietly but firmly, grabbing Simon's hand and pulling him to his feet.

I'm pretty sure she's not talking about the Poem on an Autumn Leaf kind. I just nod and smile as they leave, walking in perfect step.

Ludo and Peroxide Eric's snog gets epic, noisy, handsy. A cackle rings out across the dining hall: Etienne Gracey and his "guys," probably cracking up at Frog Girl Heidi playing third wheel.

I could let it bother me. Like, I could let myself feel a bit gutted that no one noticed I was looking a bit gloomy in the first place. But it's no big deal. I have a boyfriend, after all. A very kind, thoughtful, useful one.

Message from: gingerbread_ed <gingerbread_ed@frogmail.com>
Subject: nothin' good

song for my baby:

don't be blue, i'm thinking of you, thinking of us two, we could live in a shoe, or an igloo? yeah an igloo would do, so long as i'm with you, coo coo cachoo.

bilbo says i should give up the songwriting. feh, what does he know.

think i'm nearly as blue as you about the little leaf. i can't believe betsy has to close it down. no more gingerbread! hate hearing you so upset. sorry i'm not there with my arms around you. to keep you warm in the igloo, yeah? ;-)

h, miss you like you wouldn't even believe,

ed

Message from: dai_fawr <dafydd.wyndavies@goldfinch.ac.uk>
Hey dude,

Whoa, the Little Leaf is closing? That sucks.

Hugs will be provided for Ryder anyways. I could do with one myself.

Later dude.

Message from: gingerbread_ed <gingerbread_ed@frogmail.com>
hey dai,

yeah, it's closing, unless business really picks up. maybe you guys could all start eating insane amounts of cake or something?

surprised she didn't tell you. but i guess you're all busy with this musical thing, right? she told me you got a big role, congrats man.

ed

Message from: dai_fawr <dafydd.wyndavies@goldfinch.ac.uk>
Hey dude,

Big role is right: I'm the comedy fat guy, just like last year.

No insane amounts of cake for me: have to stay pretty for my pretty boy. But maybe we can come up with something: can't have Ryder getting all doomy on us, that's what Fili's for . . .

Later dude.

OAK.

HEY.

The Dai-mood is starting to make a little more sense. I've seen the script: Malcolm Malvolio is a big dork who thinks Olivia fancies him, and winds up dressed in fairy wings, chained on a cage-dancer's podium, trying pointlessly to impress her when she's totally out of his league. We're definitely laughing at him, not with him.

I suppose it's the kind of thing Big Dai got a bit too used to. And now he's Buff Dai, able to pull hot Henry types — and it makes no difference.

Another tiny envelope winks onto the screen before I can hit REPLY.

Message from: dai_fawr <dafydd.wyndavies@goldfinch.ac.uk>
Hey dude,

God, I'm embarrassed now. Don't tell anyone what I just wrote, yeah? Not even Ryder? I'm not usually this pathetic, I swear.

Later dude.

I want to hug him then and there. I mean, I could be a touch miffed that he doesn't want to tell *me*, but maybe it's a guy thing. Ed's totally the kind of easy-to-talk-to mellow type anyway. He'll be much better at this stuff than me.

Message from: gingerbread_ed <gingerbread_ed@frogmail.com>

hey dai,

no biggie, mate. i'm good at keeping secrets.

ed

ludovica_b: hiiiiiiiiiii ed

gingerbread_ed: hey

ludovica_b: OMG me so sad

gingerbread_ed: yeah

ludovica_b: no more gingerbread :(

ludovica_b: is heidi ok?

gingerbread_ed: hard to tell

gingerbread_ed: she's pretty tough though

ludovica_b: yeh I spose

ludovica_b: we will look after her for you!!!!

gingerbread_ed: cool

gingerbread_ed: know you're busy with this play and all

ludovica_b: OMG yes!!!

ludovica_b: did she tell you?

ludovica_b: I have the best part

ludovica_b: well not the BEST part

ludovica_b: but I get to tie up Dai in chains, LOL

gingerbread_ed: sounds like eric's a lucky guy

ludovica_b: OMG!!!

I keep on waiting for Fili to drop Ed a little note, too, even if it's just to mope over the loss of the ultimate Goth brownie supply and not about me at all. But there's nothing. I sit next to her in Chemistry, in French, in Prowse's stupid English class ("No, Heidi, writing someone else's poem onto a literal autumn leaf does not count: Do it *again*, please."). I doodle little pictures of cupcakes and gingerbread men all over our *Martine's Day Trip to Paris* comprehension worksheet, while she fills in all the answers as usual. But she goes on sighing, and working, and melts back into the two-headed hand-holding creature Filimon at the end of each lesson.

It's hard for Ed not to take it personally. He's a sensitive soul, after all.

But he's definitely not the only one feeling left out. I catch up with Ludo and Dai on their way to the Performing Arts Block, and a certain gloomy figure is noticeably absent.

"No Fili?"

"She's probably busy with her new best friend, *Yuliya*," says Ludo, savagely swinging her bag at the wilting rose-bushes that line the path.

OAK.

HEY.

Detective Heidi wasn't seeing things after all: Maybe there really is a problem between Fili and Ludo.

"But I thought you liked Yuliya?"

I don't think I've ever seen them have an actual conversation, but then I'm not sure Yuliya's managed that with anyone.

Ludo tosses her hair and says nothing. I look to Dai for further info, but he just shrugs.

"Don't look at me. I only live here," he says wearily. Then he seems to stop himself, as if remembering something, and suddenly there's a broad grin on his face, and he's wrapping an arm round my shoulder as we walk. It feels different from the squashy Big Dai hugs of the old days, but it's still nice.

A second later, Ludo's stringy arms wrap round my middle to give me a squeeze, too.

"What's that for?"

"What, we can't give Ryder a squish for no reason?"

"Yeah, HEIDI, can't we give you a squish for no reason?"

"Or, you know, because we thought you might be entitled to some squishing?"

Apparently all Ed needs to do is throw in a little request, and they jump right in. I sort of want to cry, it's so sweet of them.

"It must be SO hard, doing the long-distance thing," sighs Ludo, giving me an extra tight squeeze. "You here, and your gorgeous Ed so far, far away . . ."

I wriggle a bit, feeling awkward, and not just because we're trying to walk and hug at the same time.

"It's not so bad, really," I say, casually. "We talk a lot online. I mean, I miss him, *obviously*. Like, loads. Tons. Several tons. But then you don't see your guys 24/7, either, do you? Eric's mostly in different classes from the rest of us, and he's often off doing his own thing. And Henry's off with his Upper School mates, like, all the time!"

I feel Dai's arm across my shoulder slacken and fall away.

Ludo stumbles along beside me, oblivious, still hugging, but Dai shoves his hands deep in his pockets.

"You're not worried he's going to go off with someone else, then?" he mumbles, staring down at the path.

OOPS.

Brilliant: I take the most belongingest moment imaginable, and manage to turn it into a paranoia fest.

I fumble and babble something about trusting the people that you're with, and only spending time with people you can rely on to be honest, but the awkward feeling keeps getting worse and worse the more I talk. And then we're at the door of the auditorium, and they head inside for their cast rehearsal, Dai still looking glum.

I'm still hanging around outside feeling ten kinds of guilty when there's a skittery patter of footsteps on gravel.

It's Fili, late for rehearsal, hundreds of skinny braids streaming out behind her as she runs. She skids to a stop beside me, her pointy pixie boots all dusty, looking sweaty and embarrassed and entirely un-Fili-like as she tries to catch her breath.

"I don't think you missed much," I say. "The others only just got here. And Venables is always late."

She nods, still breathless, resting her hands on her knees.

I sort of want to say something else. I just don't really know what.

She looks up at me with her big brown eyes. I wait for the eyebrow to rise, for the familiar friendly smirk to mock me for just standing there like a dork. But it doesn't come. She opens her mouth to speak, but maybe she doesn't know what she wants to say, either, because nothing comes out.

"I still hang out by the garages at the end of the day," I say, eventually. "On the balance beam? Just till my mum turns up. You know, if you were ever bored around that time, wanted to hang out . . ."

There's the tiniest hint of a smile at the corner of her mouth. And then she's in through the auditorium doors with a flash of silver rings.

I spend the rest of the afternoon feeling oddly nervous. But when I head around the back of Stables and see Fili perched there on the end of the balance beam, just like last year, I can't remember why. I just grin, walk a little quicker, and clamber up beside her.

"So how was rehearsal?"

She nogs, lifting her hand and tilting it from side to side, in that "it was OK" motion.

"How's Yuliya?"

"Good." She considers it some more. "All right anyway."

"You two getting on well?" I say, casually. "Spending a lot of time together?"

Another nog.

"Because it's nice, I think. If you do get on. With her being your roommate and everything."

I'm getting the patented Fili eyebrow raise now.

"I just mean . . . well, Ludo sort of noticed you haven't been wanting to hang out with her so much, and, you know, if that's because you'd prefer to hang out with Yuliya, then . . ."

I stop myself. I'm babbling, when I meant to be ultra-subtle and sneaky and Mycroft Christie-ish about the business with Ludo. And anyway the eyebrow is gone. She's not looking mocking now. She's looking . . . frightened?

I know Ludo's wrath can be pretty scary and involve hair pulling, but that seems kind of extreme.

"If I tell you something," Fili says, very softly, "do you promise to keep it a secret?"

I blink as her brown eyes settle on me, very, very serious all of a sudden.

I'm the ultimate secret-keeper, I want to tell her. I'm keeping the biggest secret of all, all day, every day. You can totally trust me.

"Of course," I say. "Whatever. If you don't want me to, I won't tell a soul."

"Not even Ed?"

She's still staring at me.

"Not even Ed," I say, shaking my head a bit too quickly. "I mean, not that he'd say anything. I mean, who would he tell? And you could totally trust him to keep it a secret anyway, even if there were anyone he could tell. Which there isn't. But, you know, I wouldn't be going out with him if he were that kind of a person, would I? Like, you wouldn't be going out with Simon if he were that kind of a person, would you? You go out with people because you trust them, and they'll be honest . . . and for other reasons as well, obviously, like, you know, the obvious ones . . . but you wouldn't . . . I mean, you in general, not you personally . . . I mean, none of us are . . ."

I end up putting my hand over my mouth as if I'm scratching my nose, because it seems to be the only way to make myself shut up. But it's already too late. I don't even know which bit of my gibbering did it, but Fili's closed up again. She's looking down at the ground, her fingertips pressed together in her lap.

"Sorry," I say. "Go on. Say whatever you were going to say."

She presses her palms even harder together, as if she's trying to crush something flat between them. Then she hops off the beam.

"Go home, Heidi," she says, eyebrow turned up to eleven. "Go home and talk to your precious Ed."

And then she's gone.

I don't really know what just happened, but apparently it's not Ludo that Fili's got a problem with: It's Ed. Precious Ed. Gorgeous, thoughtful, *imaginary* Ed. I have no idea how I'm meant to fix that.

Or when I'll get the chance. The next afternoon I'm back to waiting on the balance beam, all on my lonesome.

Betsy does her best to pretend everything is normal on Saturday, but we both know it's not.

"Don't, sweetie, you're breaking my heart," she says, as she catches me wistfully stroking the frilly bit on the bottom of my apron.

"You're breaking my . . . intestines!" I pout back. "You have no conception of the trauma my insides go through the rest of the week. I have a clinical need for chocolate chips and teacups come the weekend. And I think I may be genuinely addicted to your carrot cake."

"That'll be the teaspoonful of crack cocaine in every slice," comes Teddy's sleepy voice from the kitchen out the back.

Betsy throws an apologetic glance at the customers (all two of them), scrubs out today's Daily Wisdom (NO, WE DON'T DO CAPPUCCINO! OR ANY OTHER MONK-BASED BEVERAGES), and replaces it with OUR CARROT CAKE DOES NOT CONTAIN ILLEGAL NARCOTICS.

Teddy ducks out of the kitchen, adds "*Today*" underneath, grins, and sneaks back out of sight.

"At least I've got a few months to detox, right?" I offer, weakly.

Betsy smiles, but I can tell her heart's not really in it. She drops three mugs before 10 A.M., and spends the lunchtime non-rush flapping at the smoke alarm with a wet tea towel, while a tray full of black, forgotten scones stinks out the kitchen. By midafternoon, she escapes upstairs with a headache.

"She really would be staying if she could," says Teddy, propping floury arms on the counter. "*We* would, is what I mean. If the finances added up. Hey, just look around? Not exactly rushed off of our feet."

I hop onto one of the stools at the counter, and dangle my feet as I look around. He's not kidding: The summer rush is well and truly over. I think I've drunk more tea than I've sold today. Even the Finches are avoiding us: Instead of last week's cheery Sofa of Sex posse, there's only a handful of Upper School preppie boys — Henry included, though he's only given me the briefest of nods before going back to his friends.

They laugh. A lot. Henry looks comfy, relaxed. Henry rests his hand on Jonas Bergdorf's shoulder. Henry leaves it there for quite a while.

Detective Heidi thinks: Maybe Dai's right to worry.

"Gives us time to work on our project, though, right?" says Teddy, knocking on the counter to drag my attention back. "The artwork? Costume designs? Earth to Heidi, anybody at home in there?" This time he knocks on my forehead, tap, tap, tap.

"Sorry," I mumble, coughing a puffy cloud of flour out of my face. "Distracted. Sorry."

I wait for a snarky comment, but Teddy chews on his lip, and dips his curls toward me.

"Seriously, dude, what's up? You OK? You seem a little . . . blah."

I'd been looking forward to updating Betsy on the Gingerbread Ed situation today, but that's not going to happen: She's got enough on her plate. And I kind of need someone to tell, someone completely uninvolved in Finch-world. The resident prettyboy already knows I'm Heidi the Superdork Who Has To Invent Her Own Lovemonkey: I don't think I can be more humiliated than I am already.

So I mumble a vague explanation of my woes (while deconstructing and remaking my left braid for cunning eye-contact-avoidance purposes), and wait for him to mock my pathetic girly problems. Or pull a Betsy, and sensibly point out all the ways I'm making it worse. Instead, he just looks thoughtful.

"Wow," he says. "Lot going on up in that noggin of yours, huh? And I thought my life was complicated."

I'm about to eyeroll at the comparison, but then I clock the thoughtful look properly, and realize I'm not the only one with reasons to be blah. Me, I'm used to packing up and moving on all the time. Doesn't make it easy. And I've never really had a life — or a Lovely Safak — to leave behind.

"Sorry, I guess all this 'maybe moving to the other side of the world' thing must be pretty strange for you, too, right?"

He nods slowly, chewing his lip and looking all pretty and sad at the same time.

"Well, if you want to de-blah yourself, I'm here," I say. "And very discreet. Promise. I won't even tell my imaginary friend."

He laughs, shoots me a sweet smile, then shakes himself and slaps the counter.

"OK, enough! Since the both of us are feeling only ninety-five percent shiny right now, we need distractions. And sugar. And — thank you."

He adds the last bit over his shoulder, while rustling up a plate of triple chocolate cookies. It's cute.

"Same to you," I say, as he lays out his sketch pad between us. "Seriously, though — you sure you want help me with this stuff? It will be used for dubious Finchy purposes."

Mucking about with costume designs sounds like a great way to take my mind (and his) off all the weirdness — but the Lovely Safak goes to Mendip Road round the corner, and Mendies and Finches don't exactly mix. There's a sort of ongoing war, in fact. But I suppose Safak's a bit above territorial fistfights in the Victoria Park fountain. Anyway, Teddy plucks a pencil from behind his ear.

"I'm all yours," he grins.

"Okeydoke. But I warn you: My research into nineteen eighties' style has left me mentally scarred, so yell out if the primary colors are starting to make your eyes bleed."

The Mothership and Dad Man have been taking me on a trawl through their teenage record collections over the last few nights. Watching those huge wobbly black discs spinning round, crackling and skipping as an *actual needle* scraped across them, was kind of horrifying. The Mothership and Dad Man are very, very old, the needle seemed to say. They'll probably die soon. They'll want you to play "I Fell In Love With a Starship Trooper" at their funerals.

I've got some pretty clear ideas, though. I was going to talk them over with Simon, but whenever I see him he's with Fili, and since I'm feeling more than a little awkward over the Precious Ed business, giggling about matching jumpsuits and neon socks with Teddy is definitely more fun. I write down the cast list, and wave my arms around trying to describe a Flock of Seagulls hairdo. Teddy draws lots of squiggles. Every now and then, we sell a cup of Oolong.

By closing time we've invented a new cake (Rubik's Battenburg), learned the dance routine from Adam and the Ants' "Prince Charming," and decided to make Dai wear roller skates in the opening number.

"Working hard, are we?" says The Lovely Safak, breezing through the door in a floaty flowery dress.

"Hell, yeah!" says Teddy, blowing her a kiss. "I had to listen to Heidi sing. If that's not work, I don't know what is."

"I did get sort of carried away," I mumble, fiddling with my apron frill as she wafts over to sit beside me.

"Ridicule is nothing to be scared of!" Teddy shouts tunelessly, striking an Adam Ant pose. Then he shuffles all our scribbly papers together. "I'll get these ready for you in a week or two, yeah?"

"Oh, you don't need to do anything fancy. I can just take them as they are," I start to say, but he shakes his head.

"Nope. I promised designs, so designs are what you're going to get." He leans across the counter, conspiratorially close. "Don't tell anyone, but I'm kind of enjoying myself."

"Aw, I love it when he geeks out," Safak says, ruffling his curls. "Now shimmy, boy! Movie starts in twenty minutes."

Teddy grins, and hurries upstairs.

"Thanks for cheering him up," whispers The Lovely Safak, beaming at me over her shoulder as she glides after him.

I make a quick mental note: Must give Ed more ruffleable hair.

○ ○ ○

Usual term-time service continues at the Finch. Dad Man catches Etienne Gracey climbing up the fire escape to Stables. There are room searches on the emokids after someone writes "I ♥ PUNK ROCK" in petrol across the herb garden and sets it alight at 3 A.M., followed by room searches on the Gardening Club after someone adds "U ♥ MILEY CYRUS" in weed killer underneath. The Mothership leads assemblies on what to do if you find bags of puke in your roommate's wardrobe. Jo-Jo Bemelmans gets sent home over a "medical issue" (also known as failing the random drug testing).

And they add an extra hour into the schedule for ITP, because Integrating Through Positivity with Mrs. Ashe and her helmet hair is obviously going to fix all that.

Our group struggles through the usual moronic role-play scenarios (Henry was bullied by Jambo Colley for being Polish: *And how would you respond, Henry? Well, Mrs. Ashe, I'd probably begin by saying, "I'm not Polish."*), and writing a "contribution" of ten things we like about the Finch. That fills up the first hour well enough, as everyone chews the ends of their pencils and looks blank.

And then we end up out by the lake, Henry, Fili, Peroxide Eric, Yuliya, Jambo, Honey Prentiss, Brendan Wilson, and me, all sitting in the cold October sunshine at the Circle of Peace. That's what Cooper always called it anyway: this tucked-away little spot surrounded by trees, looking out over the lake. Everyone else calls it The Logs, because it's some logs.

I have a horrible moment of panic when I think she's going to pull out a guitar with a rainbow strap and make us all Sing Our Pain, but apparently we're sticking to a different one of Cooper's lesson plans.

The Secrets Box.

Brendan makes the inevitable filthy comment, while Ashe hands round paper and pencils, and explains it to the newbies who didn't play this game last year. Everyone has to write down a "secret," or a thing they're worried about, completely anonymously, and drop it into this big cardboard box, and then she reads them out so we can all offer our brilliant insights. She doesn't mention the bit where the secrets are usually fictional (*I'm failing Potions. My daemon is a Chihuahua, and I'm allergic to dogs. I woke up this morning and realized I was a cockroach: Is this normal?*), or less-than-complimentary (*I hate this lesson and have spent all of it thinking about shoes.*), or the once-per-term guaranteed-a-laugh crowd-pleaser: *Help! I'm trapped inside a cardboard box and people keep dropping bits of paper on my head!*

I end up chewing on the end of my pencil again. This is the first time I've done this when I actually have a real secret to keep — a really huge, gossip-worthy, Gingerbread Ed–shaped one — and there's no way I'm risking a Frog Girl–shaped future by writing that down.

But I'm a detective. Ed's been good at finding a few things out, so far. Time I started pulling my weight.

I scribble down my secret, making my handwriting look slightly less scrawly than usual just in case, then take the box from Henry on the log to my right, and pass it to Honey on my left. It makes its way round the circle, to Fili opposite me, who hands it to Eric, who hands it to Yuliya, all the way back to Ashe.

"Now, class," she says, peering at Cooper's script while holding her glasses-on-a-string away from her eyes, as if she's hoping they might get less cheesy that way. "Let's all remember how we'd like our secret to be treated, and make sure we grant everyone else's the same positive energy. Sharing is a very challenging thing to do, so let's be respectful." She opens the box, and reaches in.

"I have a crush on a teacher."

"Isn't that a bit unprofessional of you, Miss?" says Brendan.

"Thank you, Brendan. Remember, it's not important who the secret is about, just how the person might feel."

"Horny, Miss?"

"Respectful, I said, Brendan? But yes, there might be some sexual feelings involved."

SECS.

YEW.

WOOL.

That's how she says it, like it's some kind of rare medical condition. She's like a one-woman condom. No one would do it ever again if they had to listen to her talking about it first. It's probably why they hired her.

"Embarrassed?" says Honey.

We all immediately think it's Honey's secret.

"I'm just guessing. It wasn't *me*," she says, touching her cheek where it's gone pink. "Ew, disgusting."

"Afraid?" says Peroxide Eric.

He doesn't look embarrassed. Or afraid. No one thinks it's him.

I realize no one thinks it's me, either. Having a boyfriend is *awesome*.

"Good. Why might someone feel afraid?"

"They might get what they want," says Peroxide Eric, when no one else speaks. "They're worried they're not as experienced as some old dude. Classic example of performance anxiety."

There's a ripple of giggles.

Mrs. Ashe coughs. "Of course, no teacher in this school would allow such a thing to happen, Eric, as I'm sure you know. We who work in residential education are trained to manage such behavior. It's inevitable that sometimes feelings of warmth and affection toward the people who take care of your needs here arise."

I remain unsold on the inevitability of Finches feeling the urge to make sexytime with Mrs. Ashe. Especially as presumably that also applies to the Mothership.

Also, she's going to say "sexual" again. I can feel it.

"But if those warm feelings tip over into something *sexual*, then of course the teacher would gently explain that such a relationship really isn't appropriate."

"I thought sexual feelings were a beautiful and natural flowering of adulthood?" says Henry, very slowly and deliberately in a perfect impersonation.

And anyway we know Mizz Cooper's lesson plan thinks so, because it's printed back there on her classroom wall, in pink Comic Sans.

"Well, yes," says Mrs. Ashe, shuffling her laminated response cards anxiously. "Sexuality is something to embrace, to enjoy, to never feel ashamed of."

"Unless you're doing a teacher?" says Peroxide Eric.

"I think we're getting away from the, er, *supportive* aspect of the sharing experience." Mrs. Ashe opens the box quickly and pulls out another slip of paper.

"I think we'll allow that one to remain a secret," she says, crumpling it up. That'll be Brendan, then. She reaches in for another, slower this time in case it bites.

"All the time I'm with Girl A, I can't stop thinking about Girl B."

I scan the group. Unless certain people have unexpected announcements to make, the possibilities are pretty narrow. Brendan could be a contender (sympathies to Girl A if so), if he didn't write the other one. Could be Jambo. But only Peroxide Eric is leaning back with his arms folded across his chest, the tails of his gray coat draped neatly over his log, big strappy boots stuck out straight for balance, whistling.

He's not even trying to hide it. It's like he *wants* us to know.

Peroxide Eric's cheating on Ludo — or at least thinking about it.

I'm not an expert, but if Ed did that to me, I'd be . . . well, surprised, mostly. But then I'd be angry. Or upset. Or both. If I were Ludo, I think I might be a little bit devastated. I'm a little bit devastated myself.

I look over at Fili, but she's in default gloom mode. Her face is blank: not a flicker of a reaction. It's like she's somewhere else entirely.

I glance back to Eric, and realize he's watching me again. Smiling at me working it out, maybe. Maybe just smiling.

"Goodness, what a romantically inclined lot you are," says Ashe, attempting to giggle and sounding a bit like a clubbed seal instead. "Would anyone like to share how they think this person is feeling? *Politely*, please, Brendan?"

Brendan closes his mouth.

"Well, I hope they feel dirty," says Honey. "And guilty. And that they break up with Girl A, because that's, like, mean."

If Cooper were here, we would now be validating Honey like she'd never been validated before. As it is, the flashing neon sign of Personal Issues goes ignored. (We all know she's talking about Etienne Gracey anyway. That guy gets around.)

"Yes, well, I think perhaps you could work on your empathetic skills there, Honey. But I see your point of view, certainly. It doesn't seem like a very kind way to behave."

"So that person *should* feel dirty?" says Henry. "Won't

that get in the way of embracing and enjoying the sexual flowering?"

"I don't think *dirty* is quite the right word, Henry, no. But one really ought to limit the quantity of the . . . embracing."

"By how much, Miss?" says Brendan.

I glance over to Peroxide Eric again, catching his eye without meaning to. He holds my gaze for a moment, still smiling, then looks away. He's got tattoos on his arms: inky hand-drawn ones, all the way up his right arm from his wrist. I'm just looking at his tattoos. That's why I caught his eye. He's looking at me looking at his tattoos.

"I don't think you can catch diseases from Girl B just by thinking about her, Mrs. Ashe," says Henry, very seriously.

"No, certainly not. But thinking can lead to all sorts of bad behavior."

"You recommend we stop thinking?" says Fili, slowly.

"No, no, obviously thinking is very important. But just try not to think so much about each other. Like that. In that way."

"Because it's dirty?" says Henry.

Mrs. Ashe puts on a spectacular performance of the show I like to call "Accidentally Dropping the Prompt Cards for a Distraction." Mycroft Christie does the same thing with the banknotes in the auction house scene of episode 2.3, "South by Southwest," so I can't really fault her.

"Let's have another secret, shall we?" Ashe says, once they've been gathered up. "Now then: *All my friends seem to really like my new boyfriend, except for one. How can I change that person's mind?*"

My toes curl up inside my shoes.

OK, so it's sort of pathetic. But I want everyone to love Ed, and Fili obviously doesn't, and I don't even know why. Plus it just so happens that if it turns out she only likes people's boyfriends if they're from Düsseldorf and enjoy wearing lederhosen on the sly, my boy might find himself with an unexpected makeover.

My eyes go to Fili before I can stop them, waiting for her to look up and nail it: see through me like the super-amazing brainy awesome beautiful best friend she is, who would totally love Ed if she'd just give him the chance. But Fili's weaving the tassely bits at the end of her black scarf together, sighing as if this secret isn't quite up to her standards. Just like with Peroxide Eric and Ludo: like she doesn't care about any of us at all.

I'm totally failing at standard undercover detective protocol, so I clamp my lips together and perform a perfectly casual inquiring sweep of the circle. Who, me? I'm just one of the group. I'm simply wondering whose this one is, like all the others.

"Next!" says Brendan.

"Now, Brendan, we're not here only to talk about *sexual* feelings. Friendships are just as important. So let's think about how this person might be feeling, hmm?"

"Lonely," says Henry. "They might have to sacrifice an old friendship to keep the new one, without any guarantees the new one will last. And they can't even talk about it to the people they care most about."

I turn to look at him, startled. He's Henry Kim: I can't imagine he's ever been lonely. But he's looking down at the grass, and for a deranged millisecond I think this must be *his* secret, not mine.

Suddenly, Henry hanging out with Jonas and the other Upper rich boys looks a little different.

"Scared?" says Honey. "Because, like, if her friends don't like her boyfriend, maybe really that means they don't like *her*?"

I hadn't thought of that. That wasn't the question I meant to ask.

Honey pinks up again. "Or him. Her or him. I don't know, it's not me, yeah?"

But now I'm looking at Fili, and it sort of makes sense. I'm not upset that Fili doesn't like Ed. I'm upset because Ed is me, and even though she doesn't know that, that doesn't mean it doesn't sting.

ITP: Insanity Through Paranoia? Or Ickily Truthful People?

"So what might this person do, do we think, to deal with these feelings?" says Ashe, taking off her dangly specs and waving them so the chain goes twinkly in the sun.

There's a long silence.

"There's nothing they can do," murmurs Fili eventually, still plaiting the ends of her scarf, and looking, quite firmly, at the ground. "People like who they like. It's not always convenient. It's just how the world is."

UChat

gingerbread_ed: hey ludo

ludovica_b: hi bb!

gingerbread_ed: you ok?

ludovica_b: better than ok

ludovica_b: :-)

gingerbread_ed: do i even want to know?

ludovica_b: omg prolly not!!!

ludovica_b: think I'm in luv

gingerbread_ed: oh

gingerbread_ed: you still seeing that eric guy?

ludovica_b: seeing a lot of that eric guy

ludovica_b: ;-)

ludovica_b: sorry to disappoint you bb, hahaha

Message from: gingerbread_ed <gingerbread_ed@frogmail.com>
hey dai,

h told me you and your fella are being really sweet to her, so thanks,
mate. think she was feeling a bit blue about one of her friends? probably
nothing really, you know what girls are like. or maybe you don't.

sorry, that was probably kind of rude.

ed

The penthouse, at night. Dashing gentleman detective Mycroft Christie observes, while his lovely assistant Miss Heidi Ryder paces up and down, deep in thought.

MYCROFT CHRISTIE: I believe I'm supposed to do the pacing up and down, deep in thought, around here.
HEIDI: Shush. It's all right for you: Your problems are fun, involve killer assassins from The Future, and can generally be solved in forty-two minutes. Mine are a bit more complicated.
MYCROFT CHRISTIE: I've had my share of experience in the affairs of the heart, my dear.
HEIDI: I noticed, Mr. Dead Girlfriend of the Week.
MYCROFT CHRISTIE: There's no need to be personal. Not all of them died. And some of them turned out to

be evil. Granted, that's not a resounding advertisement for my taste. But might my other area of expertise not be wholly irrelevant?

HEIDI: Beard-growing? Coat-wearing? Being kind of pompous?

MYCROFT CHRISTIE: I was referring to the art of detection. It seems to me that you have a case. Several, in fact.

HEIDI: Huh?

MYCROFT CHRISTIE: Case number 1: Miss Ludovica Bianchi and her gentleman friend with the wandering eye.

HEIDI: But what am I supposed to do about that? She's really happy, and I don't want to mess that up. But she should know if Peroxide Eric is being a git. Although he might not be, and then I'd have ruined all her happiness for no reason. But then if it is true and she finds out later that I knew, then she'll hate me. So what's a good detective meant to do? Tell Ludo? Yell at Peroxide Eric?

MYCROFT CHRISTIE: Or determine the identity of his Girl B?

HEIDI: Ooh.

MYCROFT CHRISTIE: Find the girl, find the crime — or lack thereof. If Girl B is blithely unaware of Peroxide Eric's interest, then he's done nothing more than think about her — and Ludo need never know.

HEIDI: And if Girl B turns out to be Tarty McSlutcakes who's been doing the nasty with him round the back of the gym, I'll tell Ludo, right after I've given him a kick in the jewels?

MYCROFT CHRISTIE: Your ladylike turn of phrase is charming, my dear. But yes, it appears you have the general idea. Now, case number 2: Mr. Dai and Mr. Henry.

HEIDI: I can't figure out if they're the perfect couple or a total disaster. They're so cute together! But now Dai's gone and convinced himself that Henry's just waiting for the opportunity to dump him for a never-been-fat upgrade, and Henry has no idea that's why he's being weird — but since Dai *is* being weird, maybe Henry *is* just waiting for the opportunity to dump him. Except I sort of assumed he was way too nice to do something like that.

MYCROFT CHRISTIE: Perchance a detective might make further inquiries into said niceness?

HEIDI: *Perchance* I could. Some gentle interrogation of Henry, to check he's not going to turn out to be Evil Boyfriend of the Week and break ickle Dai's heart? Followed by knocking their heads together till they go back to being adorable?

MYCROFT CHRISTIE: After your success at finding your own perfect partner, I dare not doubt your matchmaking skills, Miss Ryder. So, finally, case number 3: Fili.

HEIDI: Um. Yeah. I thought she was just a bit wrapped up in Gothboy, and too busy to talk to Ludo. Or Ed. Or me. But she's not too busy: She just doesn't want to. I think she hates me. Though now Dai says she's being a witch to everyone.

MYCROFT CHRISTIE: And why might that be?

HEIDI: I have no idea. OK, case number 3: Figure out *if* Fili is being a witch, *why* Fili is being a witch, and fix both of them. Somehow.

MYCROFT CHRISTIE: Excellent.

HEIDI: I do actually have homework to do, you know. It's all right for you: You've never had to investigate three sets of relationship shenanigans *and* create a scale model of the Manor for your art coursework.

MYCROFT CHRISTIE: Not especially surprising, when one considers that I'm a fictional construct and this conversation isn't real.

HEIDI: Don't harsh my metatextuality, man. I've got imaginary detective work to do.

Recipe for Magnificent Detective Activity

INGREDIENTS:

1 intrepid girl detective
1 imaginary boyfriend
1 Peroxide Eric (potentially cheating)
1 Henry (potentially evil)
1 Fili (potentially a witch)

METHOD:

• Put on The Coat to create appropriate mental atmosphere.
• Place girl detective in traditional surveillance role: tailing suspects, questioning witnesses, etc.
• Deploy imaginary boyfriend as sleeper agent.
• Return Leftover Squad to happy state of contentment (add/subtract boyfriends to taste; avoid inclusion of Frog in recipe at all costs).

In theory, being the Finch's resident detective should be easy. All the major players are conveniently located within a small, mostly inescapable location. My surveillance doesn't need to take place behind a folded newspaper or wearing a funny mustache, because I'm undercover as Heidi, aka "that girl with the braids," who will never be suspected to be the glamorous Miss Ryder, PI. Thanks to my network of informants (aka the Mothership, who has all the school schedules in her filing cabinet, and Dad Man, keeper of the keys to everywhere), I can track each of my targets' expected daytime locations down to the last minute.

EASE.

EE.

In practice: not so much. It's kind of entertaining, lurking behind pillars to eavesdrop, lingering at the end of the lesson to put my calculator away amaaaaazingly slowly, even doing the "Oh, look, my shoelace is undone, I must stop to tie it up immediately" trick (although either I'm freakishly gifted in the shoelace-tying department, or they don't come undone in real life anywhere near as often as you'd think). But it turns out that knowing that Henry's got French first thing on Wednesday morning isn't much use, when I'm over in Math making Venn diagrams about hamster ownership. Lurking in the lunch line taking careful note of what kind of potatoes Peroxide Eric is having today (with masterful subtlety) doesn't actually reveal the innermost workings of his mind. And when it comes down to it, much as I like the idea of sneaking up the Manor stairs into someone's bedroom, rifling through their drawers, and finding the envelope marked IMPORTANT CLUE — only to thrillingly hear someone approaching and have to hide under the bed — doing it for real is a no-go. I can't really steal Dad Man's keys. I'd sneeze. I probably can't hide under Fili's bed, because the dorm rooms have the kind with drawers in, and even if I could fit in the drawer, the drawers are probably already full of shoes and homework folders and stuff. Do real people even send each other letters anymore?

Then there's the time already taken up with sitting in PAG Artistic Team meetings nodding a lot while Venables gets all sweaty about whether the stage wings should be covered in pink glitter or silver satin, failing to find words that rhyme with "autumn," concocting persuasive reasons why I can't eat the Mothership's broad-bean puree, working at the Little Leaf (which is still deathly quiet, apart from me and Teddy expanding our Adam and the Ants dance repertoire to include dandy highwaymen) — not to mention the fact that all kinds of significant detection-worthy action must be going on all evening, after I've gone home.

Even when I am up there at the top of the hill, I have to be careful not give myself away, by lingering too hopefully around Fili, or asking Dai too many questions about Henry, or watching Peroxide Eric to see if his eyes are wandering in the direction of Scheherezade or any other potential Tarty McSlutcakes. So far I've only really noticed him snogging Ludo a lot — and occasionally staring at Fili, which would be funny except he's only staring at her because I am, while she's making it hugely obvious she'd prefer me not to exist by firmly looking the other way. Meanwhile, Dai's virtually moved into the gym, and Henry always seems to be off doing actorish things in the auditorium, both of which might be Of Grand Significance or Kind Of Meaningless.

Even Mycroft Christie would be struggling with this caseload. It's not doing a whole lot for my glowy sensation of belonging, either. I could have an entire pond full of slimy things in my Bubble Wrap bag right now, and not one of them would notice.

But like Mycroft Christie, at least when I head back to headquarters, I have a sidekick I can really rely on.

By day, I'm Agent Ryder, slightly useless girl detective — and by night, I sit under my desk lamp, grin at the squishy eye of my gingerbread boy, and set him to work. Life would be simpler if he'd get on with it all on his own, but sometimes a girl has to give her boy a little push in the right direction. He's not just there to cheer me up, now: He's a man with a mission. *It's a dangerous job*, Gingerbread Ed seems to say. *But it's all in a good cause, and if anything goes wrong, you can always eat the evidence.* I'm not completely convinced about that last bit (he's starting to look a bit dusty, after all, and he doesn't smell quite as yummy as he did before), but it's definitely more worthwhile than quadratic equations.

hey,

so, uh, yeah. life sucks. i suck. i even tried writing a new song called "everything sucks" but — guess what? it sucked.

h: miss you like singing in the rain, maybe you miss me, too?

ed

OK, so I'm being a bit naughty, inventing an argument, and it's not what you'd call subtle, but hey, Ed's a boy. Boys aren't supposed to be subtle. (Besides, I bet the part where we made up was adorable. He probably sent flowers. Or chocolate. *Definitely* chocolate.)

UChat

ludovica_b: omg eeeeeeeeeeeeeeeeeeed
gingerbread_ed: hey
ludovica_b: you ok bb?
gingerbread_ed: yeah
gingerbread_ed: i was kind of blue earlier but i'm ok now
ludovica_b: what happened?

gingerbread_ed: i talked to h, we're fine now

gingerbread_ed: you know, relationship stuff

ludovica_b: lol yes

ludovica_b: know that stuff ;)

gingerbread_ed: yeah?

ludovica_b: yeah

gingerbread_ed: everything ok?

ludovica_b: yes

ludovica_b: no

ludovica_b: kind of?

gingerbread_ed: anything i can do?

ludovica_b: aww ur sweet

ludovica_b: must be nice havin a bf like u

gingerbread_ed: so she tells me :-)

ludovica_b: lol

gingerbread_ed: thought you all had nice bfs there

gingerbread_ed: h seems to like that henry guy

ludovica_b: yeah he's cool

gingerbread_ed: yeah?

ludovica_b: he has such good clothes!!!

gingerbread_ed: ok

gingerbread_ed: what about the guy who is seeing fili?

gingerbread_ed: simon?

ludovica_b: don't know

ludovica_b: don't really see fili anymore

ludovica_b: think she doesn't like me :(

gingerbread_ed: oh

gingerbread_ed: why's that?

ludovica_b: omg, heidi talks lots about boys

ludovica_b: don't you get jealous?

gingerbread_ed: no

ludovica_b: haha

ludovica_b: don't believe you!

ludovica_b: i will have to keep my eye on her

ludovica_b: lol

AW.

Message from: dai_fawr <dafydd.wyndavies@goldfinch.ac.uk>

Hey dude,

Ryder giving you a hard time? Lemme know if you want me to give her a kick. And I've got a spare seat over here in the Loveless Puppies Rest Home if ya need it.

Later dude.

Message from: gingerbread_ed <gingerbread_ed@frogmail.com>

hey,

um, no, no h-kicking required. was just crossed wires: thought she was going to call, she was mad at me for not calling, etc. etc.

you really loveless? downer. h is always telling me how sweet henry is over you.

ed

Message from: dai_fawr <dafydd.wyndavies@goldfinch.ac.uk>
Hey dude,

That's nice to hear. If the gorgeous sod could just SHOW me that every now and then, I wouldn't complain though, know what I mean?

Later dude.

"You spend too much time on that computer, babes," says the Mothership, whenever she pops up to the attic. "Talking to that boyfriend of yours, are we?"

I must look horrified, because she smiles, and gives me one of her stiff little hugs.

"Parents aren't as daft as they look, you know," she says, smoothing down the tufty end of my braid. "Especially not ones who are teachers. We do hear things. And I know you're growing up: Your father's always saying you should be doing more teenage things. I think it's nice. So no need to be so secretive, babes, yeah?"

Secretive is my middle name. (Mycroft Christie, episode 1.1. Though obviously it's Karen, really. Mine, not Mycroft Christie's. We never find out his real one, so maybe he really is called Mycroft Secretive Christie. Or Mycroft Karen Christie. He's from the future: They might go for that sort of thing.)

"So, is it anyone I might recognize?" she says, quite casually, like she's not at all dying to know.

My eyes stray automatically to the desk, where Gingerbread Ed is listening to the conversation, with a very smirky cast to the squishiness of his eye.

"Maybe," I say, quite casual, too.

Then I make homeworkish noises until she gives up and goes downstairs to do something alarming with beetroots.

Gingerbread Ed: so delicious, even the Mothership can't wait to meet him.

It does add to the list of things I need to watch out for up at the Finch, though. Agent Ryder's efforts at covert surveillance are rubbish enough, without looking over my shoulder to check the Mothership's not watching me watching Henry watching Dai, with a funny little smirk on her face. Or when we're coming out of French, and Ludo waits till we're right outside Dad Man's little office when he's on the day shift to start bellowing at me.

"OH MY GOD, Heidi, do you need, like, glasses? You're, like, STARING at people."

I give Dad Man a little wave as we go past, and I pretend not to notice the way his head sticks out of the doorway to see who I might be staring at. Especially when his eyes widen in curious surprise, and I realize that Etienne Gracey just happens to be walking ahead of us.

But there's a line of people all streaming out of the back entrance, down past the lake, toward the auditorium.

"Where are we going, Ludo?"

"Duh. PAG meeting? It's been on the notice board FOREVER? Oh my God, maybe you do need glasses."

I think I might need more than glasses. I've got a lurking feeling Venables is expecting a bit more than my Flock of Seagulls hair mime, but that's about all I've got to offer. Teddy promised he'd nearly finished doing whatever it was he was doing to our scribbly notes to transform them into "designs." I'd meant to bike over to the Little Leaf to pick them up before this meeting. I've been a bit preoccupied with important detective activity, though: PAG and notice boards haven't really been top of the list.

Somehow I don't think Detection is going to cut it as an excuse for Venables.

Ludo drags me into the Performing Arts block regardless, and pushes me over to where the rest of the Artistic Team is at work. Simon's there already, looking like a pale little twig with hair, wearing what looks suspiciously like Fili's favorite black jumper: the one with the little holes in the sleeves that you can put your thumbs through. He gives me a wispy nod as I join him, ducking out of the path of Miyu Sugawara, who's staggering under a giant sparkly sign reading ORSINO'S! She adds it to the piles of painted backdrops and huge wooden props resting against an upright piano: martini glasses twenty feet high, the world's brickiest mobile phone.

Panic status: moderate, increasing.

Maybe this could be *Twelfth Night: The Naked Musical!*?

The sliding walls of the auditorium are pushed back, along with most of the seats, and the cast are all lined up against the back wall doing stretches for . . . some reason that probably makes sense if you are the theatrical type. Or Scheherezade just wants everyone to see her in a leotard, which is just as possible. Dai's doing sit-ups, sweatily. I can see Yuliya, long arms in a graceful arc over her head, and Ludo behind her with her tongue trapped between her teeth, face scrunched up in concentration, trying to replicate it. Fili's sitting off to one side, reading her script, and glancing up every now and then at Simon, as if she's checking he's still there (which of course he is, watching her with a sort of dopey dreamy expression). I'd be thinking how sweet and coupley they were together, if I wasn't just a little bit mad at her not liking how sweet and coupley me and Ed are (or would be, if dopey dreamy expressions were possible when your eyes are made from icing).

Ludo still has one arm in Yuliya-pose, but the other starts waving madly, and through the misted-up window I can see Peroxide Eric, huddling out there in the drizzle with his coat collar flicked up, smoking a cigarette. That would be sweet, too, if I wasn't wondering whether his little smirk was from seeing Ludo or thinking about Girl B. I narrow my eyes, switching back into Covert Detective Genius mode, to track down the true direction of his gaze. I'm not being Covert enough, though: He's just looking at me.

Then I notice that Henry isn't even here, which might explain why Dai's looking quite so miserable (unless that's the sit-ups), which gets me thinking all kinds of not-cute things.

The foyer doors bang, and Venables comes flying in, his half-unbuttoned shirt going alarmingly see-through from the wet, and his usual cloud of hair sticking damply to his head. He does a pantomimed look of surprise at finding people already there.

"Sorry, guys, you know how it is, crazy schedule! So much to do! But it looks like you've got it all in hand, yeah? Great. Brilliant. Cast, I'll be right with you. Just got a little bit of business with my dear old friends over here. So. Props guys, looking good. See you found that glitter paint, Timo. Fantastic. Brilliant. Love it. Now, then: costume department?"

Simon and I exchange nervous looks. Well, I look nervous. With him, it's a bit hard to tell.

The doors bang again. This time it's Henry, looking perfectly untroubled by the weather, carrying an umbrella and a huge cardboard box.

"Delivery for the Hungry Performers' Club!" he shouts, making his way over to us and bringing a tide of curious Finches behind him. "Chocolate Rehearsal Cupcakes! Fudgy Date Loaf! And there's a special order of Yogurt Raisin Oatbars in here for the health-conscious gentleman who likes to watch his waistline — for no apparent reason, I might add?"

Dai beams, pinkly, as Henry gives him a wink. From the

looks on their faces, I think that qualifies as "showing" Dai he cares.

I stare at the box, curious, as Henry swats people away, holding it up over his head and promising goodies after they've worked on the opening number.

"I took the liberty of phoning in a standing order at the Little Leaf," Henry murmurs to me, thumping it down on top of the piano at last. "Couldn't help but notice that business seemed to be a little slow, and, well, I've never been in a production that didn't run more smoothly with the aid of chocolate. I hope you don't mind?"

I grin. I don't mind. I don't mind to the point of possibly skipping about like a loony. Betsy must be thrilled, and Henry — as if there were really any doubt — has officially proven himself to be Not Remotely Evil.

"For you," Henry adds, lifting a cardboard tube out of the box and throwing it over to me. "Teddy said you'd left it down there by mistake?"

OO.

ER.

My hands are kind of shaky as I open up the tube and pull out a big sheaf of curled-up sheets of paper. The costume designs: It has to be. I can feel Simon's breath on my arm, standing close. And as the crowd of cake-hunters fades away, Venables appears, too, his hands on his hips, eyes wide with expectation.

I wish I had time to look them over first. This could be a total disaster. Part of me even wants them to be rubbish, so

I'll know there's no way Teddy can be going to art school: no way he'll be heading to Chicago, and taking Betsy with him.

But they're not scribbly rough cartoons, like the ones Teddy drew in the Little Leaf. Not anything like those. They're proper designs: *Project Runway*-style swoopy figures with mutant rectangular heads and triangles for hands. I can see all my original ideas, but he's built them up, twisted them about, made them into something beautiful. The cast are split into two groups, like I suggested: Niteclubbers in sharp neons and silver flashes; New Visitors in flouncy pirate shirts and military jackets, all navy blues and red ribbons. There are splashes of color and tiny handwritten notes on the costumes for the twins, Viola and Sebastian (matching military jackets: hers powder blue, his pale pink), to show that when she's pretending to be a boy, she wears a white stripe across her nose, like Adam Ant — just like I'd wanted.

Then Simon tugs the Feste costume to the top, the one which will be Fili's: a Pierrot, a sad clown with painted tears, all very David Bowie circa *Ashes to Ashes*, somehow all very Fili at the same time. It's exactly how I pictured it, only about four thousand times more brilliant.

Teddy is a star. A pencil-wielding angel. A cupcake with legs. I'm going to do all the washing up for him next Saturday; that's how awesome he is. But still, I feel so proud of myself. I mean, I didn't do the clever bit, the pretty-making bit, but I did the thinking-up-stuff part when I've never done anything like that before.

"Ace," says Venables, impressed to the point of almost shutting up.

He also says I'm amazingly talented, which is where I get fumblingly and awkward and start trying to explain that actually that would be someone else. But then he starts going on about responding to the inherent cultural subversion of the post-punk era, exploiting the androgynous themes, and how my faux-militarism is an amazing critique of Thatcherite economics. The rest of the Artistic Team starts to crowd round and make cooing noises, patting me on the back. I go sort of blushy and giggly and un-Heidilike, and the chance to explain that I hadn't really intended any of that, and actually the impressive parts weren't me at all, kind of passes by.

Simon's too busy still gazing adoringly at the Pierrot and her jaunty little hat to mind anyway. I feel a little stab of envy, watching him as one black fingernail traces the curve of the painted face, his lips slightly parted. No boy has ever looked at me like that.

And then she's there, at my side, stepping in as the rest of the Artistic Team go back to their glitter paint.

I wait, a little breathless, for her reaction. She's not going to leap around squeaking like Ludo would, obviously. But I know she's going to love it. It's impossible not to love it. And even though it wasn't actually me who drew it, she's going to hug me, and give me one of those rare smiles, and case number 3 can be forgotten about because everything's perfect.

She blinks. Flicks her eyes up at Simon. Flicks them back to the sketch. Flicks them to me, and holds them there. No smile. Then she sighs and takes Simon's hand, walking away looking even sadder than the Pierrot.

Heidi Ryder PI gets a little flashback to ITP: to gloomy Fili who doesn't like Ed. *You like who you like, that's just how it is.*

And I get a little shiver, and I realize it's not that I'm angry. It's that I miss her.

to: bloodwinetears@letterbox.com
from: gingerbread_ed@frogmail.com

dear fili,

this is probably a really weird thing to do, but heidi seems kind of upset about whatever it is that's happened between you. though i don't really know what that is. anyway she doesn't know i'm writing this, but i have her passwords in my laptop (that's how i got your e-mail address) and i thought i'd just write and say that she seems kind of sad about it, whatever it is. and that she'd still really like to be your friend. and she misses you.

i think she doesn't really know how to say it to your face, though, so I decided to send this.

hope it isn't too weird,
ed (heidi's boyfriend)

Dear Ed,

I know how you must feel. I feel very strange writing to you like this, too. It helps me to write things down when I'm feeling like this, shape the feelings into words, find the order in the chaos. I might not even send this message, but I feel calmer already now I'm sitting still, alone, still alone. Talking, without having to speak out loud.

The thing of it is, I'm a terrible person. I don't think Heidi would like me too much, if she really knew what I was like.

So it's a very kind gesture, you writing on her behalf, but I think I deserve to meet this darkness alone.

Fili

WOE.

UH.

I was enjoying Ed being Mr. Sensitive. I hadn't really expected him to turn into my own private Secrets Box.

I've always thought Finches — even Leftover Squad Finches — had a sort of shell that I wasn't born with, that made them somehow unbreakable. But it looks as if we're all equally squishy under our skin. Even Fili: Fili the Unique,

Fili the Tower, not Fili Who Does What It Says On Her Tin, Yawn, Next Please. She might look and sound like another Flick Henshall, but we kind of laugh at Flick Henshall and her Epic Emopain as Expressed Through Her Poetry/ Wrist Warmers, and no one laughs at Fili.

Maybe no one listens to Fili, either. I thought I'd tried, but I didn't, not really: I got distracted by my Precious Ed. I watched her and her doting Gothboy, and maybe possibly perhaps I was a little bit jealous, and I didn't realize that she could have a perfect non-imaginary boyfriend and still feel lost.

I want to wake up the Mothership, and make her drive me up the hill so I can give Fili a hug, and tell her whatever it is, I'll understand. But Heidi doesn't know about this stuff. It sounds like Fili doesn't want her to, either.

That hurts. But I need to be grown up and non-whiny about it, because Fili's the one who matters right now.

to: bloodwinetears@letterbox.com
from: gingerbread_ed@frogmail.com

dear fili,

i'm really glad that you wrote to me. not that i'm glad about what you wrote, obviously, because you sounded really sad, and even though obviously we've never met i wouldn't want that for you. but it sounded like maybe it helped to tell someone, and i'm happy i could be that person. heidi told me that sometimes you feel blue, but it's different hearing you describe it. like i can see it from the inside a little better now, or something.

i'm sure heidi wouldn't hate you, if you wanted to talk to her. i hope simon's being supportive and boyfriendly, too? but you can always write to me if you prefer. i know what you mean about writing things down being a way of getting things out of you. so you can write to me whenever, and i won't share any of it with anyone unless you ask me to, i promise.

i hope you're feeling better anyway.

ed

The penthouse, on a dark night. Mycroft Christie is seated at his desk, delicately sipping a cup of tea. His youthful associate, Miss Heidi Ryder, does not have any tea. She is not very pleased about that, but cannot be bothered to go all the way downstairs to make some, talk to the Mothership, stand in cold kitchen, etc.

MYCROFT CHRISTIE: So, Miss Ryder. How goes the investigation?
HEIDI: Horribly. Or brilliantly. It's a bit hard to tell. I've definitely found some stuff out.
MYCROFT CHRISTIE: Very good. Although I understand your colleague Mr. Hartley has done most of the work?

HEIDI: Yes, but he is actually me. Try to keep up.

MYCROFT CHRISTIE: It is all rather confusing, you know, even for a time-traveler like myself.

HEIDI: Tell me about it. I keep forgetting which one of us is meant to know things.

MYCROFT CHRISTIE: Try keeping World War Five under wraps, my dear.

HEIDI: Four. World War Four.

MYCROFT CHRISTIE: (chokes slightly on tea) Yes. So. Progress report?

HEIDI: Case number 1: Ludo and Peroxide Eric. Have interrogated her and gathered valuable evidence. No Girl B suspects as yet. Propose further interrogation of relevant witnesses, and possibly hitting Eric on the head with something heavy.

MYCROFT CHRISTIE: Excellent. Case number 2?

HEIDI: Dai and Henry. Can confirm that Henry is *not* evil, that Dai does really like him, and that the two of them are kind of ridiculously adorable. Propose gently squishing them together, until they definitely see it, too.

MYCROFT CHRISTIE: I'm positively moved. And case number 3?

HEIDI: Um. That's the horrible bit. She's not a witch. She's just really sad. About . . . something.

MYCROFT CHRISTIE: Proposed course of action?

HEIDI: Feeling really guilty for thinking mean things about her? Followed by crying?

MYCROFT CHRISTIE: Or, perhaps, confrontation?

HEIDI: Definitely can't do that. She says she doesn't want me to know. I might make it worse, if she thinks she can't even talk to Ed about it. And maybe I don't want to know what the problem is. I just want it to go away. Could I borrow your Time Bureau guest pass from episode 3.9 and just go back to when we were friends?

MYCROFT CHRISTIE: I think you'll find I'm dressed in the blue pinstripe suit and have completely perfect hair, meaning I'm Mycroft Christie from somewhere in the middle of season 2.

HEIDI: Oops. Bad fangirl. Don't grow that beard, yeah?

MYCROFT CHRISTIE: Might you, perchance, be changing the subject away from the emotionally distressing topic of Fili to something silly with which you feel more at home?

HEIDI: Yes. Which is a bit pointless, since you'll already know that.

MYCROFT CHRISTIE: It's getting confusing again. You really should stop being quite so many people. Dressing yourself up as others. Wearing a different costume. Playing a new role?

HEIDI: You're being kind of weird.

MYCROFT CHRISTIE: I'm hinting. You'll work it out in a minute.

HEIDI: Dressing up? But I'm not wearing a costume for PAG; I'm just designing them. Or pretending to anyway. I don't even dress up for . . .

MYCROFT CHRISTIE: Halloween?

HEIDI: Ooh.

MYCROFT CHRISTIE: Isn't that rather soon, Miss Ryder?

HEIDI: Yeah.

MYCROFT CHRISTIE: And wouldn't a certain fond-of-black-clothing person be the ideal person to ask for costuming assistance, thus offering a fine opportunity to casually drop in on said person and say hello?

HEIDI: You're a bit good, you know that?

MYCROFT CHRISTIE: Unfortunately, I do. But I have it on good authority that my overwhelming self-belief is all part of my charm.

Mycroft Christie sits back in his chair and looks unbearably smug, if also quite snoggable. Miss Heidi Ryder takes the opportunity to stick out her tongue and steal his teacup.

Recipe for a Spectacularly Scarilicious Halloween

INGREDIENTS:

Fili, keeper of the stripy tights
Dai, formerly known as Mr. Big, now known as Mr.
  Beloved
Ludo, shiny happy person
Agent Ryder, Undercover Genius
Handcuffs
Pumpkins, plastic bats, fake cobweb spray stuff, etc.

METHOD:

• Mix all ingredients in the Little Leaf café.
• Hug till everyone is all right again.

○ ○ ○ ○ ○ ○ ○ ○ ○ ○ ○ ○ ○ ○ ○ ○ ○ ○ ○ ○

Special Agent Heidi has been working hard on Operation: Simply Belonging. Not on her World Map displaying the distribution of coffee growers versus coffee wealth, or a certain Poem, or even the costume designs for the musical, which is allegedly the talk of the staff room ("Didn't even know you could draw, babes. You made me feel ever so silly."). But a cunning plan is underway, and the foundations have been laid. Henry and Ludo have already been provided with the relevant equipment, stolen from Venables's props cupboard. I'm well on my way to restoring the Leftover Squad to happiness.

All I need now is to distribute one last item and sort out *my* outfit for Halloween at the Little Leaf. Betsy might have adopted the tea and biscuits but she's still an American when it comes down it. I've seen the photos from last year: There's going to be some serious festive decoration going on, not to mention a whole new menu. Me turning up dressed as a Schoolgirl Waitress isn't going to cut it.

Usually the Mothership heads straight home after classes on Fridays, but (uncannily, almost as if some clever person arranged it) Dai's asked for some extra swim time (which, strangely enough, Henry might have had a text suggesting he goes to watch), so I've got a window of an hour or so. I flutter my eyelashes at Dad Man, and he fake sighs, pretending to look the other way as I sneak up the huge Manor staircase to Ludo's room.

She has a single, which is lucky for whoever might have ended up being her roomie, because the Ludo approach to decoration is insane: every inch of wall covered in photos, postcards, stickers; every mirror draped with necklaces and beads; desk and chair invisible, reachable only by excavation party with laundry basket. Tonight it looks as if a small explosion may have occurred and destroyed the wardrobe. There are more clothes than I think I've ever owned in my entire life, piled up on her bed. I'd assume it was for my benefit, or maybe some consequence of the Girl B scenario, if it hadn't looked exactly the same last time I'd sneaked up here.

"So we're going for, like, American Halloween, where you don't have to be all warty," Ludo explains, holding up multiple sparkly, un-Heidilike items. "You know, you can be a slutty nurse, or a slutty cat, or a slutty . . . slut."

"Maybe I want to be warty," I say, as she drapes a pink feather boa around my neck and pouts at my reflection in the mirror.

"Oh my God, Heidi, nobody *wants* to be warty. You should let go, you know? Lose the big coat, show a little skin! We could take pictures, send them to your Ed. Or are you worried he'd get jealous?"

"He'd probably laugh," I say, imagining a squished icing eye crinkling up in amusement. "Besides, he likes me being . . . me."

I see her face, reflected next to mine, go still for just a moment. She's smiling but in a sad sort of way.

PAW.

LOO.

DOE.

Dating someone as perfect as Ed does make it hard on everyone else, I guess. Even if Peroxide Eric weren't possibly doing the dirty, he'd still struggle to measure up.

Ludo pokes through the selection of stretchy sparkly things on the bed, which wouldn't fit me anyway, though she's much too sweet to say so.

"I don't really have anything warty," she sighs.

"Well, maybe not warty. But witchy. Traditional spooky stuff. Hey, you know who'd have that stuff? We should go and ask Fili."

The casual "I only just thought of this and haven't been planning it at all" tone doesn't quite come off, but it doesn't matter: Ludo just flops onto the pile of clothes on the bed.

"Good luck with that," she says, tartly.

I think about arguing with her, but there's not much point. I think I only wanted her to come with me so I wouldn't chicken out. Or to make sure I wouldn't be the only unwelcome one.

I head up the top flight of stairs alone anyway, and hesitate outside Fili and Yuliya's bedroom door.

Part of me hopes she won't answer, but there's a thump, and the door opens.

Simon.

He's not really supposed to be upstairs in a Manor bedroom.

Then again, neither am I. And the chickeny part of me is sort of relieved. I'm here to just gently prove I'm still Fili's friend, more than anything. It doesn't need to be a big dramatic scene, with weeping and guilty confessions.

Fili's curled up on her black and silver bedcover, eyebrow

shooting up as Simon shuffles back to let me in, and I mumble my explanation. It feels so odd, seeing her and knowing things I can't say. It's like episode 1.10, "Insight," the one where Mycroft Christie can suddenly read everyone's minds, and it turns out to be kind of inconvenient and upsetting. Except I don't have to wear an Ugly Magic Ring to do it.

And maybe it's Ed who's got the Ugly Magic Ring anyway, because I can't figure out what she's thinking at all as she sighs and waves me toward the wardrobe, instructing me to help myself.

"You *are* coming tomorrow?" I say, poking through the black shirts, and the black skirts, and the ... other black skirts. "To the Little Leaf? For lunchtime? There's this theme for dressing up," I add, taking the wrapped-up prop out of my Bubble Wrap bag and throwing it to Simon. "Everyone's doing it."

"OK," says Simon, nodding through his wispy hair, then looking to Fili. "OK?"

Fili shrugs. "If that's what everyone's doing," she says softly.

She doesn't sound exactly pleased about it. But they'll be there at least. And Operation: Simply Belonging's Project Pumpkin can't possibly go wrong.

॰

Betsy does not disappoint.

The rest of town is getting by on moldy-looking pumpkins with a few triangles cut out of them and the occasional five-year-old dressed as as a witch (and getting some harsh fashion critique from the local emokids sitting on the war memorial). The Little Leaf, on the other hand, has transformed from a weird-looking place into . . . a slightly more defined weird-looking place. You can barely sit down for rubber spiders. All the usual cakes come with jammy bloodstains and sinister new names. Today's dunkable biscuit is a range of Unhappy Faces with grumpy and/or scary expressions carved into them (and, thanks to a morning's giggling, individual names: My Little Dead Pony, Mr. Sad One-Eye, Mouthless Pete). The Daily Wisdom reads THE ZOMBIES ARE COMING: *ENJOY A CAKE NOW, BEFORE YOU CRAVE NOTHING BUT HUMAN FLESH!*

Betsy's dressed as the Starbucks Mermaid, in shimmery green with two tails tied to her hair and a necklace made from coffee beans. Teddy is Jack Skellington, the Pumpkin King, with The Lovely Safak in a red wig and blue face paint as his Sally. I've cheated a little bit, and gone for an ultra-Gothic take on Wednesday Addams, on account of the hair making it somehow inevitable.

The rest of the Leftover Squad aren't doing too badly, either. Fili, Simon, and Peroxide Eric in his big gray coat are dressed as usual, while Ludo's in a tiny sparkly number that must be freezing, but Dai and Henry have stuck to the brief exactly and are wearing matching pajamas with arrows drawn all over them in marker pen. And each couple is wearing the required accessory: a big chunky pair of handcuffs, delivered by Agent Ryder as the central core of Project

Pumpkin. I might not know who Girl B is, why Fili's so sad, or whether Dai really believes Henry likes him, but I reckon a little enforced romance might just make everything a little happier. If I could be handcuffed to my Gingerbread Ed, I'd do it in a shot.

It seems to be working so far. Dai and Henry look completely delighted to be unable to escape each other. Ludo and Peroxide Eric have theirs around their ankles, meaning they keep falling into each other's arms. Fili and Simon don't technically seem to need the help, obviously, but I'm hoping it might help Fili to *feel* less alone.

"I'm guessing you had something to do with this?" whispers Mermaid Betsy in my ear as they awkwardly troop in, tumbling onto the Sofa of Sex and its circle of armchairs.

"We're the Goldfinch Escape Committee," yells Dai, giving Betsy a wave, and dragging Henry's arm along for the ride.

"On the run," adds Henry. "Don't report us to the authorities. We're never going back up that hill!"

"Not till tonight anyway," says Ludo, peeking out from under Peroxide Eric's sleeve. "You are coming, aren't you, Heidi?"

I make my "huh?" face.

"Flick Henshall got released from the clinic," says Henry. "Apparently someone thought the best way to welcome her back was to throw a party."

"It's going to be AMAZING? Like, all the Upper School are going to, like, CAMP at the lake? And have a bonfire?

Eric's going to spike the drinks and everything. It's going to be, like, TOTALLY SPESH."

"It's a Halloween party really: The Flick thing is just so the Screws won't close it down." Dai looks at me. "Sorry, no offense to your dad."

"None taken," I say, glancing over at the Bloody Bakewells and wondering how many of them I'll need to take home for bribery purposes.

"Please come? We can get ready together. I'll do your makeup. We could dress up all over again! PLEASE?"

"Seriously, please?" says Peroxide Eric, thumping his free booted foot onto the table. "Or I'm going to be deaf in one ear for life."

It's a Finch party. Ludo's going to paint my face like I'm her doll. I will witness at least three people throwing up. The Mothership will probably explode at the whole idea. But we'll all be hanging out together. It's the perfect continuation of Project Pumpkin.

"I suppose I could drop by," I say, twirling the end of a braid. "But only if you all promise to keep the cuffs on?"

"She's very kinky behind that hairdo, isn't she?" says a smirking Dai.

"I've noticed that," says Henry. "Good thing her boyfriend's not here. Who knows what they might get up to?"

HELL.

YEAH.

Agent Ryder is definitely due a promotion: License to Be Awesome (and Watch Telly Whenever You Like). Girl B won't get a look in. Dai and Henry are probably about to get married. Fili still looks like she'd rather be anywhere but here, but all this happiness has to be infectious, right?

Not to everyone, though. Betsy, for all her shiny green satin, is looking distinctly unfestive. She waits till everyone's gone, and the Go Away sign has been flipped, to tell me what a really smart detective would've figured out ages ago.

"I'm sorry, honeypie, really I am," she says, fiddling with her scaly tail. "Looks as if we've got the lease on this place till December, but after that, we're gone. And even with the extra orders from your buddy Henry — which, sweetie, thank you *so* much for trying to help — well, a Saturday waitress is a luxury we can't afford. We've got to save our pennies for the trip, so, well, I'm going to have to let you go."

"I told her to fire me instead, but apparently there's some kind of law against it," says Teddy, tapping his stick-on bony fingers on the counter, looking so genuinely sad under his face paint it makes my stomach flip over.

I see Betsy nervously twiddling her big plastic rings. Safak's watching, too, in her crazy red wig. So I do a big fake sigh, smile and nod, and give Betsy a hug. She relaxes and smiles properly, for the first time all day.

"You'd better keep coming in here till we close up, you hear?"

"Course," I say, managing to not let my voice go wobbly. "After all, I get to call him Rupert now, right? Customers' privilege?"

"Oh, I think so," grins Betsy, disappearing into the kitchen to wrap up some Two-Nosed Cindys for me.

"I didn't know your name was *Rupert*!" says Safak, nudging Teddy.

"Damn, Heidi, and I *was* about to tell you how much I was going to miss you," he moans.

I feel myself go a bit pink. I think I might actually start to cry in a minute, which isn't at all the kind of thing Agent Ryder does.

"Hey, we're just hanging out watching DVDs here tonight," he adds. "I rented *Tron*; it looks like the most eighties movie of all time."

"You did?" says Safak, wrinkling up her nose.

Teddy nods gleefully.

"Seriously, Heidi, I bet you'd love it. We have popcorn."

"I think Heidi's got a party to go to up on the hill, don't you?" says Safak, a little too quickly.

"Um. Yeah, I suppose so." I'd much rather watch dorky movies with Teddy than watch Jambo puking, but Wednesday Addams isn't really supposed to sit on the sofa between Jack Skellington and The Lovely Sally. He's only offering because he knows of my tragic state of blahness. And I do have a party to go to, where they'll all be handcuffed to their beloveds, and I'll be . . . the newly unemployed dork on her own in the corner.

"I'll lend you the DVD?" offers Teddy, walking backward as Safak begins to drag him upstairs.

Betsy comes out with a ridiculously huge paper bag of leftover goodies, and I'm definitely going to cry then, so I give her another hug, shove a Miserable Ears into my mouth so I won't have to say anything, and run.

I get all my sniffling out of the way on the ride home, and once I've had a hot bath and eaten some more Unhappy Faces, Agent Ryder is back in charge. I can always look for another job, after all. Teddy really ought to go to art school, with his amazing drawings, even if it does mean after Christmas I'll have to live without a Betsy to talk to, and Teddy's lazy smile, and his curly hair, and that little twinkle he gets in his eye when he knows Ludo is breathing a bit quicker just because he happens to be walking by, even though he never says. I can drink lots and lots of tea with them until then.

MYCROFT CHRISTIE: You're handling this very maturely, Miss Ryder.
HEIDI: I know! I'm great.
MYCROFT CHRISTIE: You'll be weeping about it in the manner of a fragile girly sort later, however, correct?
HEIDI: Shush. I'm going to a party where all of my friends are being very friendly with each other, and I'm very, very happy, so ner.

I have to be a bit creative with the Mothership about quite how enormously close I am to Flick Henshall ("I'm not sure she's the kind of girl I really want you to be all that friendly with, babes."), but Dad Man unexpectedly comes to my rescue and offers to drive me up the hill when he goes to start his night shift. The Mothership gets torn between Strict Teacher and Disappointed by Antisocial Freakish Daughter modes and gives in once I've promised to call her for a lift home before 10:30.

"No sneaking off into the dorms with that boyfriend of yours," she says, kissing me on the cheek as we're leaving. "Your father'll be keeping an eye on you."

UM.

YEAH.

I picture my gingerbread boy waiting up there in my bedroom right under her nose, and by the time we're at the Finch I'm smiling again for real. OK, so I'm going to a party without him, but he's real enough for parental angst. I should go into business: new Saturday job as a one-girl imaginary boyfriend production line.

Dad Man peels off into his little cubbyhole, and I head on through Manor and back out into the gardens. It's a horrible night, windy and wet, and I skid down the muddy slope toward the lake. Thumpy bass line. Nasty smell from outdoor candles. Etienne Gracey and Scheherezade doing a vaguely slutty-looking dance around the world's least alight bonfire. There's no sign of Flick Henshall: just Timo Januscz, holding a handmade WELCOME BACK! banner, and one lonely yellow balloon.

At least I have The Coat. It might not be standard

partywear, but my Wednesday getup had jam on it. I've decided if anyone asks, it's a costume, and I've come as the world's greatest time-traveling gentleman detective who just happens to have autumn-friendly dress sense.

I head for the pavilion, where I can see a little huddle of people and the red glow of cigarette ends. Peroxide Eric and Ludo (*both* smoking: that's new) and Dai and Henry are all squashed together on one bench. Both pairs of them are still cuffed together, too, which makes me grin.

"HEIDI!"

They all try to squeeze up, and I wedge my bum in between Ludo and Henry. Need to cut back on the blue poppyseed cake if I'm going to be doing this again. See? More reasons why being newly unemployed is actually great. Really, really great.

"Warm you up?" says Peroxide Eric, blowing smoke and waving a bottle of Something under my nose.

Ludo's teeth are actually chattering around her cigarette. Henry looks an unusual shade of blue. I think my toes may have fallen off.

I take a swig. It warms me up.

I get cold again.

I'm in one of those shows where across the bottom of the screen it says SAN DIEGO, CA, but you know they actually film it in Canada. Bikini scenes with tight cold smiles. Except no one's going to yell "cut" and bring Scheherezade a goose-down anorak between lines.

"No Fili and Simon?" I say, squinting across the lake.

160

"Nope," says Ludo. "Haven't seen them since we got back."

"Lucky you," says Dai. "Looked like there was trouble in Goth paradise, know what I mean?"

"Really?" I say, at the exact same time as Peroxide Eric does. He probably doesn't mean it in quite the same detect-y way as me, though. He chuckles, though, and we're so squashed together we all have to join in, like some freaky five-headed bench beast.

"Definitely some kind of argument," says Henry. "They were very nearly audible."

I wonder if I should go and investigate. My other cases are all neatly chained to one another, after all. Fili might be lonely.

Fili might still not want me around.

Then Flick Henshall comes sprinting down the muddy hill in nothing but her bra and pants, hotly pursued by Dad Man.

A cheer goes up from the other side of the lake.

"Oops," squeaks Ludo, as the chase comes to an abrupt end.

"Oh," says Dai. "That's . . . unfortunate."

"Lucky it's so muddy; you can't see anything," adds Henry. "Though she's probably not all that bothered, come to think of it."

Dad Man frog-marches her across the slippery grass, try-ing to cover her up a bit without actually touching her. As they walk, the rain begins to wash away the mud, revealing streaks of white skin. The laughing and clapping that rippled across the water from the watching crowd fade away: All you can hear now is the wet crackle of candle wicks spitting and Dad Man's faint mumbling reassurances.

And a clinky, metallic noise, as a chain snaps, and the broken links tinkle on concrete.

The wedged feeling on the bench suddenly disappears, and Peroxide Eric is skidding across the grass in the flickery light, his big gray coat flapping behind him. Then he slips it off his shoulders and wraps it around Flick.

There's a roar of disapproval from the crowd as the streaks of white flesh disappear under the blanket of his coat. I can hear Dad Man thanking Eric as they head up the slope back to Manor, out of sight. Flick Henshall's crying now. The crowd gets bored and goes back to trying to keep the pathetic fire going.

"We would've done that," says Dai, watching them go.

"If we'd had the appropriate clothing," says Henry.

"My hero," sighs Ludo.

I look at the broken chain on the cuff around her leg, and think that there's probably a reason Ludo's not in the top set for English, with a socking great metaphor like that going unnoticed.

Could *Flick Henshall* be Girl B?

No. She's been in that clinic since the McCartney Party: Eric probably doesn't even know who she is.

Agent Ryder could take the opportunity for a little quiet snooping, though. It's not like the party is all that gripping: People are drifting away in twos and threes, back to the houses, back to where it's warm and dry. Timo Januscz lets go of his balloon, which, not being the helium kind, just trundles along the ground until it lands on the lake. I should probably find Dad Man and see if he wants some extra coffee anyway. I really should go and check Fili's OK.

The others seem happy enough on the bench, watching the balloon floating slowly across the water as if it's an artsy new commercial, so I leave them with a little wave and make my skiddy way up the slope.

Dad Man's not in his cubby, though: Peroxide Eric neither. Probably off finding someone to deal with Flick Henshall: maybe finding her some clothes.

I squelch my way down the tiled corridor and pull one of the huge heavy front doors open. It's really raining now, hard enough that the drops are bouncing in through the doorway and splashing my feet. I wipe my face, and my hand comes away smeared with black from my not-waterproof-after-all mascara.

Jori Song stands around in dramatic torrential rainstorms all the time, and that never happens to her. Real life: just rubbish compared to the telly.

Fili's just upstairs, probably. I could call the Mothership for a lift and just pop up to see how she is while I'm waiting. If she tells me to go away, at least I'll have tried.

I fumble in my pocket for my mobile, glancing up at STUART A. MCCARTNEY 1979, carved in gold on the Student of the Year board just inside the doors. His party goes down in Finch history. I suspect that future Finches will not be holding Henshall Parties to commemorate that time it rained a lot and everyone went home early.

My eyes wander across the board as I wipe more black junk off (or more likely around) my face.

And then I think my heart stops.

Actually stops.

Like a dead person.

Which is what I am.

There it is, on the Student of the Year board, carved in the wood and painted gold. There *he* is.

E. D. HARTLEY.

I pull my soaked coat halfway off and read the little name tag in the collar. *Hartley*.

Hartley, who I named Ed because it seemed to fit, somehow. Ed Hartley, my boyfriend. Ed Hartley, whose name is up on the wall of Manor, for anyone to see at any moment.

OHM.

EYE.

GOD.

One car ride down the hill (complete with Mothership lecture on the correct application of makeup) later, and I'm back in my attic, with Gingerbread Ed.

He doesn't look like a lovestruck angsty troubadour who tinkers with his motorbike, writes poetry, and misses me like a shooting star over the roof of Stables. He looks like gingerbread. Old, stale, needs-to-be-thrown-away gingerbread.

I have to get rid of him, now, right now.

I'll delete his ULife. Erase his imaginary existence. And eventually he'll be forgotten about, like that boy from my last school who stopped coming for a few months, until one day in assembly they told us he was dead from leukemia, and I realized I'd known him exactly as long as my one and only best friend in that place, but I couldn't really remember what he looked like.

Bryan Coleman — that was his name. I haven't forgotten about him after all. Crap.

And anyway, I need Ed. He's my sidekick. He's other people's sidekick, too: Ludo, and Dai, and especially Fili. Ed wouldn't just abandon them: dash off a quick "you're dumped" blog to his Heidi and never reply to any of his messages again. My Ed would never be that insensitive.

My Ed.

Me, Ed.

I can't keep him. The profile, the messaging, they aren't the kind of thing you can just explain away as Dorky Heidi messing about. It's gone too far now to be a joke. All it takes is for someone to see E. D. H. up there in the Manor, put two and two together, and Operation: Simply Belonging will be over for good. I won't be wanted in the Leftover Squad. I won't even be Frog Girl. I'll be looking back on the Frog Girl days with fond nostalgia, wishing people still remembered those happy times, before I became That Psycho Who Made Up a Boyfriend and Prentended to Be Him.

But I can't just get rid of him, either. There'll be more questions asked if he vanishes. Fili will be all on her own. I'll be all on my own.

I start up the Dread Pirate, still trying to decide. And I discover I'm already too late.

to: heidi.ryder@goldfinch.ac.uk
from: arealboy@letterbox.com

Dearest Heidi,

I've been meaning to write to you for some time but never quite mustered the courage. I wasn't sure my attentions would be welcome. I like you, you see. I might more-than-like you. I thought perchance you might like to know that. And of course, online is your preferred method of communication, I believe?

love & affection,
E

WOE.
AH.
If I was feeling shaky before, I'm a jellyfish now. My fingers are all skiddy on the keyboard as I type.

to: arealboy@letterbox.com
from: heidi.ryder@goldfinch.ac.uk

E,

Suppose you think this is hilarious. Just go ahead and tell everyone how pathetic I am then, I don't even care anymore. Thanks for taking the piss while you're doing it, though. It's really cute of you to mock me to death.

H

I sit staring at my gingerbread boy, wondering exactly how someone four inches high with sugar for eyes has managed to take over my life. Then my inbox winks at me again.

to: heidi.ryder@goldfinch.ac.uk
from: arealboy@letterbox.com

Dearest Heidi,

Did my message get mistranslated in the ether? I said I like you. I don't recall using the word "pathetic." Nor taking the piss, which I'm sure I'd recall. Do you talk to all your gentleman friends that way?

You consider me "cute," however. This amuses me. Perhaps this is the beginning of a beautiful friendship after all?

Oh, and rest assured: Your secret (or should that be *our* secret?) is safe with me.

love & affection,
E

to: arealboy@letterbox.com
from: heidi.ryder@goldfinch.ac.uk

E,

OK, you're actually freaking me out now. You want to humiliate me, fine, can't stop you, probably deserve it. Just stop with the weird "love&affection" crap, because it's kind of creepy.

H

to: heidi.ryder@goldfinch.ac.uk
from: arealboy@letterbox.com

Dearest Heidi,

I perceive you're going to play hard to get. This shall be fun.

You disappoint me, however. I thought you wanted to play detective? You must be at least a little curious. Don't I remind you of anyone, even the merest smidgen? I've been endeavoring to be obvious for some time now, in fact. But perhaps you have a selection of possible suitors from whom to choose?

Until then, unrequited as it may be at this moment, I continue to write with

love & affection,
E

The jellyfish feeling doesn't go away. But now it's a different kind of quivery breathlessness that's making me stare at the screen, rereading and rereading.

The dimly lit penthouse. Mycroft Christie, gentleman detective, is reclining on an armchair, apparently relaxing after a party: His undone bow tie is draped loosely around his neck, and he twirls a red rose between his fingers. His companion, Miss Heidi Ryder, looks equally elegant and does not in any way have eyeliner on her chin.

MYCROFT CHRISTIE: Well, this has been a dramatic evening.
HEIDI: (makes goldfish face)
MYCROFT CHRISTIE: How attractive. No wonder you've a new beau.
HEIDI: I haven't got a new beau. I haven't got an old beau! I've got . . . I don't know what I've got.

MYCROFT CHRISTIE: Then let's consider the matter in a professional capacity. What explanation could there be for the attentions of this Mysterious E?

HEIDI: OK. I see three possibilities. One: Someone found out about Ed being imaginary, and wants to torture me before they tell everyone and humiliate me into a puddle.

MYCROFT CHRISTIE: A rather arcane technique, don't you think?

HEIDI: Yeah, but it makes more sense than possibility number two: The gingerbread man suddenly came to life and decided to send me freaky romantic e-mails.

MYCROFT CHRISTIE: Hmm. While I recall being menaced by a possessed stapler in episode 3.3, "When Office Supplies Attack," I think we can all agree that wasn't the highlight of my televisual career. It wasn't terribly plausible when it happened to me, and I am, alas, fictional.

HEIDI: Well, I've always thought so. Unless . . .

MYCROFT CHRISTIE: Oh. Would I be possibility number three?

HEIDI: You do sound a lot like him. And there's the "love & affection" bit: You always finish your letters like that. And . . . now I've stepped over the line from fangirl to total frothing loon.

MYCROFT CHRISTIE: I suspect the existence of this conversation makes that point moot. Might I propose a fourth option? That this Mysterious E, whoever he might be, is a perfectly real person who likes you? More-than-likes you? Likes you enough to find out something of your tastes in debonair television heroes and to borrow a few of their charms to woo you?

HEIDI: Dude, I'm fifteen. We don't do "wooing."

MYCROFT CHRISTIE: You're blushing.

HEIDI: Am not.

MYCROFT CHRISTIE: Are too. A very attractive shade of rose.

HEIDI: Do you really think he likes me?

MYCROFT CHRISTIE: Yes, Miss Ryder, I believe he does. And painful as it is for me accept that I'm no longer primary in your affections, I suspect you might rather like him back.

HEIDI: But I don't even know who he is.

MYCROFT CHRISTIE: Indeed. Now, if only there were a talented girl detective in the vicinity to investigate . . .

Miss Ryder plucks the red rose from Mycroft Christie's fingertips, tucks it behind her ear, and shrugs on her long detective coat.

Recipe for a Tragic Breakup

INGREDIENTS:

Gingerbread Ed, soulful biker poet
Heidi, his beloved
Mysterious E, the new man in her life
A selection of long-distance relationship clichés

METHOD:

• Blend all ingredients.
• Pour the mixture into the internet, making sure it spreads evenly to all corners.
• Bake till the face of Mysterious E is revealed, like those pieces of toast on eBay with Jesus on them.

○ ○ ○ ○ ○ ○ ○ ○ ○ ○ ○ ○ ○ ○ ○ ○ ○ ○ ○

Message from: gingerbread_ed <gingerbread_ed@frogmail.com>
Subject: oh well

so . . .

looks like i'm a single guy again.

h: miss you all the same, always will,

ed

It's a risk, with HEIDI IS A BIG LIAR written in big gold letters on the Manor wall. But I need him around, and I reckon a few other people would also miss him if he suddenly vanished completely. So we're going to have a very mature and dignified breakup, where I am only a little bit lip-quivery, and Ed is very stoic and handsome and probably writes lots of songs about our doomed romance, and I'll be very conveniently available for Mysterious E to come along and sweep me off my feet (which, love him as I do, my little gingerbread boy has never quite pulled off).

I needn't have worried about E. D. HARTLEY causing me any trouble, though. The Finch seems to have plenty of other relationship gossip after Flick Henshall's party.

Message from: dai_fawr <dafydd.wyndavies@goldfinch.ac.uk>
Hey dude,

Is there something in the water? This is like the week of breakup hell. Fili and Simon, Ludo and Eric, now you guys. Henry better not decide he's got something to tell me. . . .

Anyway, sorry, mate. Who dumped who? Not that I'm going to take sides, natch.

Later dude.

Message from: gingerbread_ed <gingerbread_ed@frogmail.com>
hey dai

wow, sounds like a lot happened after heidi left that party she told me that she'd been at. hope everyone there is ok. i guess at least she'll have company, yeah?

mutual decision.

ed

 Message from: dai_fawr <dafydd.wyndavies@goldfinch.ac.uk>
Hey dude,

Ha, totally guessed it was her who dumped you. No offense. It's just always the quiet ones who turn out to be man-eaters ;)

Stay in touch, mate.

Later dude.

ludovica_b: OMG

gingerbread_ed: hello to you too

ludovica_b: lol sorry

ludovica_b: am just surprised!

ludovica_b: i thought you and heidi were like forever love

gingerbread_ed: aw, thanks

ludovica_b: love sux anyway

ludovica_b: i hope you were nice when you split with her

ludovica_b: didn't like call her an ugly in front of everyone or anything cos that is mean

gingerbread_ed: no

ludovica_b: though bet you would not do that

gingerbread_ed: not really my style

gingerbread_ed: is everything ok?

ludovica_b: not really

---

to: bloodwinetears@letterbox.com
from: gingerbread_ed@frogmail.com

dear fili,

i suppose you'll probably hear this from someone else anyway, but heidi and i have broken up.

i wanted to let you know that i'm still here as a friend, if you want someone to talk to about anything. in case you were upset about anything, maybe.

best wishes,

ed

to: gingerbread_ed@frogmail.com
from: bloodwinetears@letterbox.com

Dear Ed,

You and Heidi are breaking up? I'm honestly surprised to hear that. But then love is complicated, isn't it? I thought my life would be instantly perfect if only I knew someone loved me. I miss being that naive. But the garden of love is a thorny threshold. Even roses bite.

You might have guessed: I'm not having the best time of it romantically myself. But being alone is all I deserve. Please don't feel you have to jump in and tell me I'm wrong, either: I'm not the girl you think I am. I promise you. But then who is?

Fili

to: heidi.ryder@goldfinch.ac.uk
from: arealboy@letterbox.com

Dearest Heidi,

When I mentioned the notion of "playing hard to get," it wasn't intended as encouragement. Ignoring me will not change how

I feel about you: It's a familiar enough situation, after all. You pass by — I hope you'll notice me watching — you glance my way, smile, move on.

You're quite the tease, did you know that?

I hope you're beginning to understand. This is not a joke, an insult, a childish prank. If I had the courage, I'd declare my more-than-liking to your face. Until circumstances allow, I shall have to be content with playing your game, with the rules you devised. Don't tell me you aren't enjoying the dance, just a little? I know I am. Perhaps that's why we're so perfectly suited?

I await your reply, as always, with

love & affection,
E

Finchworld is cloaked in gray fog and misery when I head up the hill for Monday morning death-by-Chemistry with Mrs. Kretschmer. Flick Henshall's back in the clinic, which means Timo Januscz is walking around like a human black cloud. Etienne Gracey and Scheherezade have apparently split up, possibly just to blend in with the current trend for relationship trauma. And so have I, though I'm so preoccupied with "glancing" at pretty much every boy who walks past (just in case they happen to have a huge flashing arrow with "E" written on it above their heads) that I almost forget I'm supposed to be half of one of the broken-ups, too.

Agent Ryder: Your mission, should you choose to accept it, is to look sad and symbolically Coatless in the manner of someone who just split up with her bloke, while also looking devastatingly attractive and available should A Certain Person happen to pass by, while also remembering to be very surprised when you learn of other people's tragic relationship woes.

Fortunately, Dai takes on the job of rapidly filling me in on the latest developments in the break before Science, informing me that it's Official Be Nice To Ludo Day, and then somehow managing to turn that into And Heidi Too within five minutes (plus a bonus "I always thought you could do better than that Ed guy anyway" to cheer me up, which it does, in ways he's definitely not really planned).

I feel a little bit guilty. OK, a lot guilty. But it's nice to feel looked after.

Ludo holds my hand very tightly all the way from Science to Geography, informing me that boys are SO horrible and stupid and we should, like, ALL be single forever, yeah?

Henry gives me a hug at lunch, rests his chin on my head, and tells me not to worry.

I keep waiting for the chance to see Fili, and break through our wall of awkwardness: to have her hold my hand and say the same things to me, so I can say them to her.

But Fili doesn't show up to any classes.

She doesn't even make it to the auditorium after school, even though the full cast is meant to be passing through to start the costume fittings.

The buzz of electric guitars thrums through my feet before I even get through the door. Inside, Etienne and the Illyrians (the artists formerly known as The Shrooms) are standing on the stage in a mess of cables and amps and pedals, shouting at each other above the fuzz. Etienne Gracey is out front, muttering "one two, one two" into a mike. Counting: apparently not his strong suit.

"So the band will appear to *hover* above the stage, you see? Brilliant!" yells Venables, waving the pile of costume sketches madly at some skinny blond guy I don't recognize. "Though of course I haven't signed it off with health and safety yet. . . . Heidi! Just telling your friend here about the plans for Etienne and company. So we'll need four more costumes. Something different, just for the band. Really visual, yeah? Sure an artistic genius like you can rustle up something special. Sketches as soon as you can, need to get the Sewing Club onto it ASAP. OK? Brilliant."

He thrusts the pile of papers into my hands, then bounds off to deal with the cast.

I seem to be nodding, as if I really can "rustle up" some fabulous new sketches in no time at all, using my fine artistic skills. But I suppose it'll give me a good excuse to drop by the Little Leaf: scour the internet with Teddy for more quality '80s moments of high fashion. Etienne would look lovely in tinfoil. Or a tiny humiliating loincloth. Unless this skinny blond guy has some better ideas?

The skinny blond guy gives me an awkward half smile, blinking fluffy hair out of his eyes.

I nearly drop the sketches.

"Simon?" I say, just as Etienne Gracey and his guys start playing . . . something. (It's definitely "Tainted Love" at the start, but then seems to take a sharp left into "Jingle Bells," followed by some kind of screemo wall o' sound that turns out to be Jules falling over the drum kit due to a mistimed scissors kick.) I'm quite grateful for the distraction, though, so I've time to think of something to say that isn't "huh?"

"You look really . . . different."

OK, maybe not much of an improvement on "huh?"

Simon performs a minuscule shrug, shuffling in his trainers, and ripped white jeans, and tight green T-shirt, none of which could possibly have come from Fili's wardrobe. Lost property bin, maybe.

"Sorry about your breakup and everything," I mumble, still kind of mesmerized by the transformation from Gothboy to Hipster Shufflemonkey.

He mini-shrugs again, eyes fixed somewhere down near my elbows.

I realize the drawing of Feste the clown is on the top of the pile: a beautiful sad Pierrot, quietly weeping. Maybe a little too appropriate. I gather the sheets together, and plonk them down on the nearest bench.

The whine of feedback comes to a sudden stop, as Henry

yanks the plug from the wall to a smattering of applause from the cast. They're rehearsing some fiddly dance step from the opening number, while Mrs. Philips from the office runs around with her tape measure. Dai's smirking over something with Ludo (possibly Scheherezade ordering Yuliya to slouch more, so she doesn't look so much taller). I find myself grinning just watching them. Operation Pumpkin didn't exactly work out, but Ludo looks happy, windmilling her arms and giggling as she stumbles into the wall.

A hand nudges my arm as the band starts up again, and I turn to find Henry there, looking weirdly furtive.

"Can't talk now, but can I catch you later?" He's actually whispering. Which, in the presence of the Illyrians, is not actually very helpful. "Secret thing. Nice secret. Sort of urgent. No, not urgent. But sometime this week. I'll find you."

Then he grins and heads back to where Scheherezade is waiting, hands on hips, yelling something about the impossibility of working with amateurs as Ludo twirls around and smacks into her. I give Dai a little wave, although he doesn't seem to notice.

The Illyrians produce another epic burst of feedback, which in turn produces more shrieking from Scheherezade, and I decide it's time to escape.

Outside it's not raining, but the air feels damp and the ground's all mushy. I skid my way across the grass by the lake, cigarette butts and broken plastic cups squashed into the mud from the party.

I'm slipping my way up the slope to cut through the Circle of Peace and find the Mothership for a lift home, when I practically fall on top of Peroxide Eric. He blends so perfectly with the gloom all around, grayish and pale and made out of yawns, just sitting on a log in his officer's coat. I haven't seen him all day: probably keeping a low profile. In fact, last time I saw him, he was chasing a half-naked Flick Henshall across the grass with Dad Man.

"Got your coat back, then?" I say.

He looks down, rubs away some of the dried mud that's still on the sleeve, and shrugs.

I wait for him to say something, but he keeps his eyes lowered, almost as if he's too shy to look up.

"So . . . you and Ludo broke up, then?"

"You heard?"

I shrug. "I've got ears."

"They hear anything else?"

He looks through me, past me, to the gray of the lake. He's nothing like the guy who sat here weeks ago in ITP, curling his lip over Girl A and Girl B. He looks nervier somehow, like a spooked horse.

Maybe Ludo yelled at him. She can be pretty terrifying when she loses it.

I ought to be on her side, I realize, all moral indignation and grrlpower and yay sisterhood! She was the dumpee. She's my friend. All I know about Peroxide Eric is his taste in hair dye and his usage of the word "bazoinkas." And that he smokes, and knows where to get alcohol, and I kind of want his coat because mine supposedly belonged to my ex-boyfriend so I've left it at home, and now it's beginning to rain.

He flicks his eyes at me, then, and I remember he asked me a question.

"I didn't hear anything else," I say.

He smiles sadly, and burrows down a little in his collar.

"What? What should I have heard?"

He stays nestled in the warmth of his coat, but his eyes track back to mine. Gray eyes: gray like the lake, gray like the sky.

"Nothing, Heidi. Nothing at all."

Would Miss Ryder please come to the departure lounge? The Clue Bus is now ready to depart.

I'm starting to think I must have been missing a lot of Clue Buses lately. Standing at the wrong stop, on the wrong side of the road, with last year's timetable.

Could Mysterious E be . . . Mysterious *Eric*?

It's kind of obvious. If I were coming up with a cunning disguise so I could wind me up for a little while, I'd probably not call myself H.

But what if he *wants* to be obvious? E's pretending to be a bit of a Mycroft Christie himself, after all. He's got to give me a couple of clues to go on.

I wait for the Mothership to drive me home in a giddy daze, waiting to be swept away from my stupid braids, from the Finch, from Heidiworld completely. I run up to the attic and read his e-mails again, hunting for more clues.

Until circumstances allow, I shall have to be content with playing your game, with the rules you devised.

Until circumstances allow.

Until after he's broken up with his girlfriend, perhaps?

Until he knows his Girl B has broken up with her gingerbread man?

The Clue Bus is now pretty much running me over, tootling *helikesmehelikesmehelikesme* on its horn. (Clue Buses can do that. Like ice-cream vans playing "Greensleeves" all wonky.)

Peroxide Eric sits at The Logs, in the cold and the rain, where I'm guaranteed to walk on my way back from the music rooms, and makes meaningful conversation of the sort I totally didn't get at the time but now seems made of purest meaning.

I definitely detect circumstances. Multiple circumstances. Circumstances coming out of *all* the orifices.

I mean, it's not exactly how I pictured Mysterious E. I haven't been thinking of Peroxide Eric in that way at all before now: He was with Ludo, for starters, and I've been completely boyfriended up for quite some time now and very happily, thank you for asking. But this isn't the same as Gingerbread Ed. This is *a real boy*: the very first real boy who has ever, in my entire life, liked me. More than liked me. He could probably have three heads, and I'd still be doing cartwheels, and Peroxide Eric doesn't have three heads at all. He's pretty cute. I mean, he's not *Teddy*. But I probably always thought he was cute. I like his coat. The hair and the piercings and the snarly way he smiles. He's got those stubby fingers from where he's bitten his nails down too much: I noticed it in the Little Leaf that first time he came in there, when he was twirling his lip stud around. You don't notice fingernails of people you aren't at least curious about. Or lips.

He'll taste like cigarettes when we kiss. I'm OK with that. It's not a deal breaker. Maybe we can discuss those patch thingies.

Maybe I'm getting a teensy bit ahead of myself.

He only just broke up with Ludo. I have Friendly Responsibilities to her: ice-cream consumption, crappy rom coms, lots of stern pouting at the mention of his name.

He doesn't want to be unmasked yet. He's *enjoying the dance*. Who is Dearest Heidi to stop him doing the woo-the-girl boogaloo?

And I don't *know* know it's Peroxide Eric. I just kind of sort of definitely know it's him.

Fortunately, I'm on excellent terms with my ex, who's pretty good at finding things out on the sly.

to: bloodwinetears@letterbox.com
from: gingerbread_ed@frogmail.com

dear fili,

sorry to hear things aren't go so well between you and that simon guy. heidi always thought of you two as the perfect

185

couple, did you know? but i suppose things are never really the way they look from the outside. they definitely weren't with me and her. i think she's seeing someone else, now, actually.

are you feeling any better? if there's anything anyone can do, just ask.

take care,
ed

to: gingerbread_ed@frogmail.com
from: bloodwinetears@letterbox.com

Dear Ed,

I'm probably not the person to ask about Heidi's present love life: seems like you know more than I do. Did she really see Simon and me as perfect? That explains a lot. I love her (I hope she knows) but she is awfully naive. I'm almost envious.

Sadness is my default setting: sorry. I emerge blinking into sunlight from time to time, but there are usually clouds in my sky. At least this time I have good reason to be dripping with self-loathing. It doesn't make it any easier to get out of bed in the morning, but the pure rationality brings its own strange sense of consolation.

I hope I'm not boring you. It must get dull, all this moping.

Fili

Message from: gingerbread@ed <gingerbread_ed@frogmail.com>
hey dai,

ok, so i feel like a dork for asking this, but i was wondering how h is? i know, i know, pathetic ex-boyfriend syndrome. you don't have to reply if it seems too weird.

ed

Message from: dai_fawr <dafydd.wyndavies@goldfinch.ac.uk>
Hey dude,

No sweat, mate. I know how it is, you get used to talking to someone every day and then suddenly they aren't there anymore, right?

She's fine anyway. Looks like she's moving on, if you know what I mean? Though I'm not exactly thrilled about the direction she's moving in . . .

Later dude.

gingerbread_ed: hi honey

ludovica_b: hey

gingerbread_ed: how are you?

ludovica_b: still dumped :(

ludovica_b: you?

gingerbread_ed: same here

ludovica_b: we should make a club lol

ludovica_b: breakups suck

gingerbread_ed: i noticed that

gingerbread_ed: so how come you and eric split?

gingerbread_ed: was he seeing someone else?

ludovica_b: don't know

ludovica_b: he better not be

ludovica_b: will have to find that bitch and cut her lol

ludovica_b: hello?

gingerbread_ed: hey

gingerbread_ed: i don't know

gingerbread_ed: can't change how you feel about someone

gingerbread_ed: better not to pretend, i think

ludovica_b: i spose

gingerbread_ed: want her to be happy

gingerbread_ed: even if that's with someone else

ludovica_b: i spose

gingerbread_ed: would be nice if you could feel like that about eric

ludovica_b: yes it would

gingerbread_ed: aww, poor ludo

gingerbread_ed: you'll find someone

gingerbread_ed: someone who makes you feel special

gingerbread_ed: someone perfect

ludovica_b: :)

to: heidi.ryder@goldfinch.ac.uk

from: arealboy@letterbox.com

Dearest Heidi,

I know your schedule is terribly full, but it's a challenge to dance this particular tango alone. Perchance you're simply so overwhelmed by my charm that I've rendered you unable to respond? If so, I do hope it's not permanent: The Heidi I've fallen in more-than-liking with is quite the talker.

Not even a gingerbread crumb of fond attention for your real boy? You're a tease indeed.

Nevertheless, you still have my

love & affection,

E

to: arealboy@letterbox.com

from: heidi.ryder@goldfinch.ac.uk

Dearest E,

OK, OK! My fond attention is all yours.

(I am *so* not a tease, btw.)

H

Mrs. Ashe's Secrets Box could get filled up pretty quickly if it accepted multiple submissions.

Did Fili always think I was naive?

If he doesn't like the direction I'm moving in, did Dai never like Peroxide Eric?

Does ickle pretty Ludo actually go round cutting people?

Does this include me?

Might I actually deserve that for moving in on her ex?

How long does the ex-boyfriend-hands-off rule apply anyway?

And have I got this whole thing totally wrong, because I totally tried to give Eric a gingerbread crumb of attention yesterday after lunch and he was the one hiding from me, and I think perhaps this is not a very secret secret now at all?

I linger in the doorway of the ITP classroom, trying to figure out what to write on my card before we embark on today's thrilling wall display construction (Things That

Make Us Happy — which apparently may only include pictures that can be cut out of Mrs. Ashe's prehistoric dodgy magazine collection, so there's going to be a suspicious absence of nipples, alcohol, and Mycroft Christie in favor of knitted baby bootees and Great Recipes To Lower Your Cholesterol). Fili, Yuliya, Honey, Jambo, Brendan, and The Ashe are flipping through the magazines; Fili using hers as a sort of face mask so she doesn't have to meet my eye.

No Eric, I notice with a little pang.

No Henry, either, until he appears, breathless, coming from a lead cast PAG rehearsal, and dropping down beside me to share his own little secret.

"Finally I get you on your own," he says, dipping his head close. "Bless him for it, Dai's not an easy guy to shake off. Anyway, you know it's his birthday in December? I want to do something. A party? But I could use a hand with ideas, and I feel like you're closer to him than anyone else here."

Another little pang. According to what he's told Ed, Dai is actually kind of narked with me right now. But I guess this is my chance to redeem myself. And I know one thing: Dai doesn't do birthday parties. Not since he was ten and he ended up celebrating by being shoved in a bin and rolled down a hill till he smashed into a lamppost and cracked his skull open. It's not a story he tells very often. Not one he's told Henry, either, apparently.

"Party? Not such a good idea. But he'd like you to do something, I bet. Actually he'd probably be gutted if you didn't. Just not anything too . . . birthdayish."

Henry nods, slowly. "Right. So, a birthday party, without a party, or any reference to birthdays?"

I nod sympathetically. "I'm sure you'll think of something?"

Then Ashe bellows at us both to sit down and do the Happy-Making Things, and Henry gets dragged off to sit with the guys.

Eric shows up ten minutes late, strolling in like he wants everyone to know he's just dropping by because he feels like it, but I can tell he's bluffing extra hard. The swagger's not so convincing if you keep your coat on like some kind of comfort blanket, and take a seat near Mrs. Ashe, where no one's going to go and join you. He keeps his eyes lowered, just darting them around occasionally, like he doesn't want to risk any eye contact.

I miss his eyes. His deep, pool-like gray eyes. But he has nice eyelashes, I discover. They're long: sort of girly. But in the good way.

And I get it anyway. I'm probably doing the same thing: not quite knowing where to look. Halfway between smiling goofily and running away.

I cover up by cutting out a picture of a severely dubious-looking bloke with a handlebar moustache, and gluing him enthusiastically to the paper, adding the caption SEXY FACIAL HAIR.

Even Fili smiles at that.

Mrs. Ashe comes over and demands I stick another picture over the caption, which starts Henry off on an

Ashe-baiting freedom-of-expression spree, followed by a lengthy debate on the sexiness of moustaches versus the sexiness of beards (conclusion: Santa Claus is one hot piece of ass). And then I find a picture of an orange teapot with purple cows on, which so genuinely Makes Me Happy I sort of have to stick it on.

We waste a little time staple-gunning the lunatic wall chart to the wall (Cooper never used to let us do that: staple guns and Finches are an unholy combo), then we're pushing the tables back to sit on the floor in a circle, because apparently Sharing is always best performed uncomfortable.

I make sure I'm sitting next to Fili, so I won't catch her eye when we get to mine. Which somehow leaves me bang opposite Eric, eyelashes and all.

OOPS?

We make short work of *My roomie is a phantom farter* (undeniably Jambo, whose roomie is Dunc The Monk and is the guy you don't stand directly behind in the line for lunch) and *My cat died and they won't even let me go home, and my sister says they're going to bury her under the croquet lawn* (Ashe: They're going to bury your sister under the croquet lawn? Honey: No, they're going to bury Pom-Pom under the croquet lawn. Us: You fail at being secret. Pom-Pom? Obviously this is deeply sad, but seriously, Pom-Pom?).

Then it's *I might more-than-like you, too*, and I'm suddenly very aware of my heart, sending all those red blobs spinning round my veins.

Agent Ryder looks casually out of the window, while also

looking very casually at everyone else, as if curious to iden-
tify the secret-keeper, while also entirely giving herself away
to the one person in the room who'll understand. Well, in
theory. Actual Ryder doesn't have that many eyes.

Brendan suggests something filthy enough to distract all
attention.

I take my chance. I make myself look up.

Eric's not looking at me.

But is he not looking at me in that effortful concentrated
way that actually is kind of the same as looking at me?

Definitely.

Mostly definitely?

The eyelashes flutter for a moment, dusting his cheeks,
then he tugs at his coat sleeves and ruffles his bitten-down
fingers through his hair. Shuffles his feet around. Half looks
up at me, then drops those lashes again. Tugs on his lip-
piercing.

Definitely definitely.

Next it's *I'm frightened to sing* (duh, Yuliya), one censored
one that makes Ashe look like she sucked a lemon and
stubbed her toe while a rat ran up her skirt, and *I wish I could
blame you instead of me*, which is universally slated for being
too successfully secretive.

And then?

Girl B is all I can think about.

And there's more eyelashing and ruffling and shuffling
and *definitely definitely* definitely.

OHM.
EYE.
GOD.

to: arealboy@letterbox.com
from: heidi.ryder@goldfinch.ac.uk

Dearest E,

I just wanted to say that unless I'm completely confused and stupid (which I really hope I'm not) then I obviously know who it is you remind me of. But you already know that, right?

If I'd known these would be the rules then I would totally have come up with better ones.

H

to: heidi.ryder@goldfinch.ac.uk
from: arealboy@letterbox.com

Dearest Heidi,

As it happens, I rather like your rules: I've always been fond of dancing. But something tells me our respective paths may cross one another quite soon.

In the meantime, it is, as always, a delight to hear from you.

love & affection,

E

Romantic entanglement with non-biscuit people turns out to be very similar to going out with Gingerbread Ed.

I'm still juggling plenty of who-knows-what-about-who-and-why, which means I spend most of my day at the Finch ducking out of sight behind pillars and doorways, trying to remember whether I'm meant to be being sympathetic, or friendly, or not being anything at all. And back at the attic, I still seem to be spending my time making up conversations with someone who isn't there. Eric might not have a squished eye made of icing or a tendency to lounge around on invisible furniture, but his being A Real Boy isn't making much difference.

I do see him in real life, of course: The Finch doesn't make for avoidability. But he's always on the edges. Lingering at The Logs, chewing his fingers. Smoking outside the music rooms, when Venables just happens to have called an emergency PAG meeting. Keeping the required safe distance from Ludo: hovering attentively enough to let me know he's there.

I kind of love the way he does that.

But it means by the time we actually end up in the same space as each other, alone, I've already had seventeen conversations with him about Gingerbread Ed and how very loveable and non-weird his existence is, and the importance of coats, and whether season 3 of *Mycroft Christie Investigates* would've been better without the Evil Wife (answer: yes). We've accidentally brushed fingertips. Held hands. Bench-snuggled. There may even have been kissing rehearsals.

And then there he is. The real thing, at the front steps of the Manor on an already-dark Friday afternoon, brooding against a pillar. Black roots starting to take over from the peroxide, slight stoop to his shoulders as if they're carrying the weight of a world or two, fingers drumming on the worn grainy stone. He glances up as I walk through the big oak doors and slam to a halt. I stand there like a dork. He stiffens against the pillar, and blinks. Eyelashes.

Eyelashes.

Eyelashes.

Eyelashes.

"So . . . uh. Hi."

I just smile back. Words are not forthcoming.

"So . . ."

He shifts his arms to behind his back, as if he needs to hold the pillar to stand up or something. He's as awkward as I am. He's more awkward than I am. I sort of miss the debonair Mycroft Christieness he has when he's being E — but then I'm not exactly feeling like the glamorous Miss Ryder right now.

"About this . . . stuff," he says, waving a hand, then putting it back against the pillar, as if he might lose his balance and slip off the edge of the world. I wouldn't blame him: I might, too. "I should . . . we should talk, maybe?'

I do the smiling thing some more. I think I fit in a nod, somewhere.

"Cool."

He squints, turning to look down the driveway. The darkness is split by bright lights as the Mothership's car rolls up to the steps. The engine whirrs: Gravel crunches under the tires. The headlights pick out his silhouette, framing him in darkness. He looks like a photograph, a poster, a still from the movie of *Eric: The Boy Who Was Suddenly Really Inarticulate but Also Sort of Beautiful.*

I may be staring.

I should say something.

"That's my mum."

Not that.

"She has to take me home now."

Not that, either.

"I won't be here all weekend. But, next week, maybe? I stay late on Wednesdays. There's a musical rehearsal after classes; The Manor common room will probably be quiet. So I might be in there, watching TV, if you wanted to come and find me, maybe?"

He blinks at me few times, as if he's deciphering it, as if he's really getting what I'm saying. He catches my hopeful little smile, and for just a moment I catch a miniature glimpse of E.

The Mothership honks her horn.

He shifts against the pillar again, resuming Peroxide Eric mode: solemn yet amused, artfully arranged.

Plus eyelashes.

It feels strange to walk into the Little Leaf as just another customer.

It feels even weirder to be in there as Heidi Ryder, soon to be girlfriended by Mysterious E. All the time me and Gingerbread Ed spent on the Sofa of Sex was made up by Betsy, after all. Me and Eric will be needing "Reserved" cards above it, with our names. So long as we don't dance around each other for too much longer anyway. The place is already starting to change, in preparation for the big closedown: The hat collection's gone from the top shelf, and the bottom half of the blackboard wall at the back has been wiped clean of all Teddy's squiggly chalk art.

Most things are the same, though: the Daily Wisdom (THE CAKE IS A LIE! *BUT YOU ARE ENCOURAGED TO BELIEVE IN THE LEMON SHORTBREAD*); Teddy sticking his curly head out of the kitchen to give me one of his insane, totally unaware smiles; Betsy gently but firmly telling me when she thinks I'm being a loony.

"Are you drunk?" she says, dropping a triple-chocolate brownie onto a plate for me with a puff of cocoa dust.

I shelve my outstandingly clever metaphorical explanation of how Gingerbread Ed is vanilla and Mysterious E is rum, and I try for something a little more straightforward.

(Maybe she's right, though. Mysterious E *is* rum, and I am tipsy from just thinking about him. Love is so weird.)

She pours us both cups of tea, frowning as she listens.

"So this other guy starts e-mailing you, and he knows all about your Ed? I mean, *all* about Ed?"

"Yep. But it's OK. He's not going to tell. In fact . . . well, we're kind of . . . getting together. Going out. Or, you know, planning to."

I fiddle with the end of my left braid and fidget. Apparently romance makes me act as if I'm about five. My first boyfriend was a gingerbread man: It's not all that surprising.

Betsy informs me I'm insanely cute, though, which seems more in line with my newfound boyfriend ability.

"Anyone I know?"

"You might have seen him around," I say, all coy and girly.

Teddy reappears from the kitchen, leans on the counter, and nicks a bit of my brownie. A good bit. A corner bit, crunchy on the outside, squidgy underneath. He even watches me while he's doing it, grinning, like he knows exactly what I'm thinking.

"I'll let you off for that on one condition," I tell him, digging in my bag for the list of costume requirements for Etienne and The Illyrians. "I kind of need four more sketches. Sort of urgently?"

"You think you can just stroll in here and demand I draw stuff now?"

"You're stealing my job, my supply of peanut butter

brownies, and my Betsy away to another country. Yes, Art School Boy, I can stroll in here and demand stuff."

He mock-sighs, and takes the list. So far, all I've got is four names, and the words EMBARRASSING LYCRA? with a big red circle around them.

"Lo-fi album cover art?"

I poke him with a pencil. "I'm a little short on inspiration, OK?"

He tips his head to one side, chews his lip, then grins, and disappears upstairs. A minute later, he returns with his laptop and a DVD.

"You want embarrassing Lycra? Ladies and gentlemen, I give you: *Tron*."

He's not kidding. Two hours of lightbikes, Bruce Boxleitner, and the total ignoring of our one and only customer later, I can confirm that I have indeed witnessed the most '80s film of all time.

AH.

MAY.

ZING.

"You certainly enjoyed that a whole lot more than Safak did," says Betsy, clearing away our empty mugs with a meaningful roll of her eyes.

I look to Teddy.

"Apparently it takes a special personality to appreciate CGI that crappy," he says, with a rueful shrug. "So we, uh, kind of decided to call it a day."

"You broke up over *Tron*?" I wrap a braid across my mouth, trying to hold in a giggle. "That's . . . definitely special."

He nods, curls bouncing gloomily. If curls can do that sort of thing.

I feel a little sad: Here's me, skipping about in romantic glee, and Teddy's doing the opposite. I feel the same every time I see Ludo, with a bonus twinge of guilt. There might be a super-cunning way around that, though: one of those two-birds-with-one-stone kind of plans that Mycroft Christie's oh so fond of. Ludo's always liked Teddy, after all. She's the kind of girl who absurdly lustable guys like Teddy always get, all swingy hair and the scent of peaches wafting from their elbows. She could be his Lovely Ludo. And if she's got her own new swoonsome lovemonkey, she's not even going to care what Peroxide Eric's getting up to.

I vaguely outline my genius idea, neatly sidestepping the part where the whole thing is not quite as noble and selfless as a genius idea might want to be.

Teddy just sort of blinks. A lot.

I suppose not everyone is into Ludo.

"It's sweet of you, hon," says Betsy, filling in the long, long silence. "But we're gone in, what, four weeks? Not really the time to be starting a whole new thing."

I sigh. She's right, of course. That's probably the real reason Teddy broke it off with Safak in the first place. And I definitely don't want Ludo to be heartbroken all over again.

"Four weeks?" I mumble, the words hitting me at last. "That's all?"

Betsy grabs my hand and gives it a squeeze. "I know it's hard, but it's not all so terrible. We get to go back home, catch up with family. Some of us like to do that once in a while, you know."

"Absence makes the heart grow fonder?"

"Exactly!"

It's not really what I meant, but then she knows that.

"Means you'll love us even more once we're gone?"

"We could kidnap her?" says Teddy, finally emerging from his blinky daze. "She'd fit in a suitcase. If we squashed her a bit."

I nod encouragingly. "I might not look it, but I'm quite bendy."

Betsy grins. "Sure there's nothing back here you wouldn't want to leave behind?"

I look round at the bright colors, the mismatched mugs, the familiar swoop of Teddy's chalked handwriting on the blackboard menu, the list of teas indelibly in my head (Earl Grey, Lady Grey, Orange Pekoe, Green . . .).

Once upon a time, back in the Frog Girl days, I might have wanted to parcel myself up and cover myself in stamps at the thought of losing this place. But I've got somewhere else to belong to now — and an E to keep me company.

I spend the night before The Big Date getting all my clothes out of the wardrobe, attempting to make my hair do something that isn't two braids (total failure), and ducking all efforts by the Mothership to "help." I feel a bit guilty, doing it all under the watchful eyes of my gingerbread boy. But we broke up ages ago, so it's not as if I'm cheating. I bet Ed would like Eric: I do, after all. Ed and E should hang out, and talk about imaginary guy things. They could invite Mycroft Christie around for poker. I'll end up one of those whiny girlfriends who is always sending "where r u?" texts in no time.

I think I might be a bit nervous. I've never actually been on a date before that didn't only happen inside my own brain.

Not that it's a date, exactly: just an afternoon, drop-by-if-you-feel-like-it path-crossing in the Manor common room. We're just both happening to feel like doing the dropping-by part at the same time.

Well, almost.

He's already there when I arrive.

He's sitting on the armrest of the Garden common room sofa, as if he's too wired to flop down into the cushions. One big boot rests on the edge of the coffee table, nudging the Finchtastic pseudosculpture of crunched Red Bull cans and photocopies on Sikhism. He's got his coat collar turned up again. It does things to his cheekbones. Good things. Very appealingly watchable things.

I watch from the door as his stubby fingers fiddle with the remote, jabbing it at the plasma screen as if infrared works better if you give it a push.

Some crappy game show plays on the plasma screen.

I should've got here earlier and set up the DVD player: Set the timer so while we were talking, *Mycroft Christie Investigates* could suddenly start playing, and we could have our first kiss to the opening credits, and then snuggle on the sofa to watch the rest. The very first episode, to symbolize our new beginning. Or maybe episode 2.13, "Chaos Theory," for the Mycroft/Jori snog that we were waiting for all along. Or . . .

Eric looks up, and sees me, and OK, I'm really not going anywhere.

"Hey." I wave.

"Hey."

"You having trouble there?"

"Yeah. Volume control."

"Probably the batteries."

"Yeah."

"It works sometimes if you take them out, and sort of warm them up with your hands."

"Really?"

"Yep. Well, that's what my dad says. Although he's probably just trying to get out of buying new batteries."

"Uh-huh."

SHUT.

UP.

"So . . ."

"Yeah."

In the multiple preshoot rehearsals of this scene, I'm pretty sure I gave myself a better script. Him, too. I pictured him playing the whole thing in Mysterious E-speak, in fact. Although his stumbling nervous thing is kind of thrilling, all dark and suggestive. I'm just stumbly and nervous, without any subtext. He gets dramatic pauses: I'm the goof who can't remember the next line.

Heidi sucks at this.

H is going to have to take over.

I come in properly, and swing my leg over the other arm of the sofa, so we're sitting like bookends. For, you know, really big books.

"So you wanted to talk?"

Oh yeah: H is all kinds of daring.

Eric shrugs. "Yeah. I figured . . . yeah. Like, you were the person I should be talking to, you know?"

"That would seem logical."

He does this sweepy eyelash thing that could stop clocks and traffic and maybe save the world.

"So . . . how's Ludo doing?" he says, fingertips softly dabbing at the rubber buttons on the remote. "If you don't mind me asking?"

I don't mind him asking. I love him asking. Gingerbread Ed was the asking type, which means the asking type is totally *my* type, and this is all destiny. Or something.

"She's OK. In the not-very-OK sense, natch. I think she really liked you. As in, *more-than-liked* you, you know?"

He doesn't smile at the reference. He just looks sad.

I kind of want to reach out and hold his hand, and for that to sort of tumble us into some kind of inevitable lying-on-top-of-one-another-oh-however-did-that-happen? thing. But this stupid bookends position (that seemed like a fabulous artistic decision at the time: We'd look awesome in widescreen) means I'm too far away for it not to involve trampling across the sofa, and probably the middle cushion would slide off halfway across like it always does, and I'd just fall on the coffee table and break it, or me.

"She'll be all right, you know. She's got lots of people looking after her."

He nods, slowly. "Yeah. I still feel bad, though."

"About moving on so fast?"

"I guess you could call it that," he says, and smiles.

His eyelashes rest on his cheeks when he does that. I should make him do that more often.

"I think it's like Fili says," I say, smiling myself. "You like who you like. You don't do it because it's convenient, or good timing, or appropriate. You just . . . feel it."

"Well, she'd know, right?"

He's looking right at me now. Those soulful gray eyes. Fingers still wandering over the remote as if they can't quite stop themselves. Little crease in his brow.

"I didn't think she'd go ahead and break up with Simon over it, though. Or if she did, at least we'd end up together. Now it's like nobody's happy, know what I mean?"

He's still looking at me, all eyelashes, eyelashes doing their thing, me nodding, listening, listening to . . .

Wait.

Stop.

Break up with . . . *Simon*?

"Anyway, you're the kid who seems to know everything around here, right? So I figured you'd know if I've got a shot."

I don't know how I'm breathing. I feel like I've eaten the sofa instead of sat on it.

"With Fili?" I croak.

"Yeah. Because, you know, we had a good time. But I hear Etienne Gracey split up with that chick with the crazy name, so, you know, if Fili's not interested . . ."

"I . . . really . . . couldn't say."

Eric sniffs, and shrugs. "That's girl-code for no, right?"

He tosses me the remote and jumps up, his coat brushing my elbow as he sweeps past.

"Tell her I'm sorry and all that. And thanks for being cool about it, yeah? Sweet."

Then he's gone, and it's just me, and the TV, and . . . that's not what I want.

SWEET.

SUITE.

AI.

LASH.

IS.

Recipe for Disaster

INGREDIENTS:

Heidi
Reality

METHOD:

• Place your Heidi in the presence of other people.
• Watch as she proceeds to not notice anything
that's going on around her, despite thinking she's
a detective.
• Point and laugh at results.

○ ○ ○ ○ ○ ○ ○ ○ ○ ○ ○ ○ ○ ○ ○ ○ ○ ○

"If someone broke your heart, babes, you can tell me," says
the Mothership, over watermelon and apple soup. "I'll give
them as much detention as you want."

Motivational: not so much.

And I'm not heartbroken. I'm horrible. I never imagined

in a million years that it would be Fili who cheated — and that's mostly because if it were going to be anyone I would've expected it to be Ludo. Or maybe myself, apparently. So I'm back to spending nights sitting at my desk, staring at Gingerbread Ed, wishing real boys were also handily pocket-sized, cinnamon-scented, and altogether less likely to make the whole world feel so meh.

I get sick of looking at his sarcastically squished eye after a while, so I turn him around and somehow knock him against the lamp. One arm snaps off. He looks even more sarcastic. I decide to take revenge and nibble on his nonexistent elbow.

It's like biting into a telephone. Or rocks. Or some other very hard thing, like diamonds, except for the vague taste of treacle, orange peel, and spices. And dust. Lots of dust. Like a sort of gray icing made from ick.

Even my imaginary boy has gone off.

A dimly lit penthouse: so dim that it's quite impossible to see the face of dashing detective Mycroft Christie as he converses with his plain and extraordinarily thick colleague Miss Heidi Ryder.

MYCROFT CHRISTIE: Truly, my dear, you have a gift for metaphor.
HEIDI: Least I've got a gift for something.
MYCROFT CHRISTIE: Might I detect a little wounded

pride behind my reappearance? I was under the impression you didn't need me anymore.

HEIDI: I thought I had an E to talk to instead. But apparently I've thought lots of stupid things lately.

MYCROFT CHRISTIE: The true identity of the peroxide-headed gentleman's Girl B was rather a surprise, certainly. But as that piece of the jigsaw slots into place, it does bring a few others along for the ride.

HEIDI: I suppose. I get why Fili was being quite so down on herself now. And why she didn't want to talk to Ludo. Or me, in case I got all judgey about her stealing Ludo's bloke.

MYCROFT CHRISTIE: And would you have "got all judgey"?

HEIDI: Um. Maybe? Just a little tiny bit?

MYCROFT CHRISTIE: Despite "you like who you like," and wanting people to move on and be happy, and — forgive me for mentioning it — rather wanting Eric all to yourself?

HEIDI: Temporary insanity. Finch flu. I'm over him.

MYCROFT CHRISTIE: Even the eyelashes?

HEIDI: I hate eyelashes. Eyelashes are horrible. From now on, I'm only ever going out with people who don't have eyelashes. Scratch that: I'm never going out with anyone ever.

MYCROFT CHRISTIE: But what of Mysterious E?

HEIDI: Mysterious E can stay mysterious. I. Don't. Care.

to: arealboy@letterbox.com
from: heidi.ryder@goldfinch.ac.uk

E,

This has been all sorts of amusing, but I'm done. Romance is for people who are better at life than I am. Go and wave your lovely affectionate bits at someone else, OK?

H

to: heidi.ryder@goldfinch.ac.uk
from: arealboy@letterbox.com

Dearest Heidi,

Shush.

With enduring
love & affection,
E

to: arealboy@letterbox.com
from: heidi.ryder@goldfinch.ac.uk

E,

Seriously. It's too tiring and embarrassing, and I'm way too pathetic for this to be worth the effort.

H

to: heidi.ryder@goldfinch.ac.uk
from: arealboy@letterbox.com

Dearest H,

You're flirting again.

My ever increasing
love & affection,
E

to: arealboy@letterbox.com
from: heidi.ryder@goldfinch.ac.uk

E,

Am not.

H

to: heidi.ryder@goldfinch.ac.uk
from: arealboy@letterbox.com

Dearest H,

Are too.

L & A,
E

to: arealboy@letterbox.com
from: heidi.ryder@goldfinch.ac.uk

E,

D2?

H

to: heidi.ryder@goldfinch.ac.uk
from: arealboy@letterbox.com

Dearest H,

It was your way with words that first attracted me, I believe.

My
glove & affliction,
E

to: arealboy@letterbox.com
from: heidi.ryder@goldfinch.ac.uk

E,

:P

H

MYCROFT CHRISTIE: I do believe, you're smiling, Miss Ryder.

HEIDI: I might be. Just a little bit. Though I still don't know who he is.

MYCROFT CHRISTIE: Isn't that half the fun? Now to work, my dear: The game is afoot!

HEIDI: Um. Yes. Whatever that means.

to: bloodwinetears@letterbox.com
from: gingerbread_ed@frogmail.com

dear fili,

how are things? are you feeling any more cheerful at all? just wondering, really, if you're OK. i know what it's like to feel crappy and alone, and not have anyone you can tell.

best wishes,
ed

to: gingerbread_ed@frogmail.com
from: bloodwinetears@letterbox.com

Dear Ed,

It's kind of you to still write: You must be the most attentive ex-boyfriend ever. If only I could inspire the same degree of dedication. I'm unworthy of it, though. Poison kisses and betrayals is all anyone can expect from me, alas.

Does that answer your question?

Fili

Message from: gingerbread_ed <gingerbread_ed@frogmail.com>
hey,

how are you doing, man? h called me tonight: sounds like you were right, she's definitely into someone else. guess that's the way it goes.

ed

Message from: dai_fawr <dafydd.wyndavies@goldfinch.ac.uk>
Hey dude,

Oh yeah, Ryder's after someone else. Don't know she's going to get him, though. ;)

Later dude.

gingerbread_ed: hey

ludovica_b: hi bb!!!

ludovica_b: missed you

gingerbread_ed: been busy

gingerbread_ed: but thanks

ludovica_b: did you miss me, too?

gingerbread_ed: of course

gingerbread_ed: how is heidi?

ludovica_b: think she is over you, bb

gingerbread_ed: she seeing someone else?

ludovica_b: mmmmaybe

ludovica_b: ;)

gingerbread_ed: that's ok, i kind of knew

ludovica_b: you have a new gf now?

gingerbread_ed: nope

ludovica_b: i thought all the good ones were taken

gingerbread_ed: maybe i'm not such a good one

ludovica_b: bad boy ed?

ludovica_b: lol

ludovica_b: i must be just your type

"So you've gone from dating a cookie to dating the invisible man?"

Christmas has come early to the Little Leaf, since they'll be missing the real thing. Betsy's rocking a Santa hat and shiny-wrapped present earrings, and the menu is crammed with snowman meringues and, inevitably, gingerbread men.

"Dressed like that, you don't get to mock me. Anyway, we're talking, not dating. On account of me not actually knowing who he is. Still."

I have explained the traumatic Peroxide Eric non-date to Betsy. Well, kind of. There may have been some editing in postproduction.

"So why don't you just ask him who he is?"

I shake my head firmly. "Against the rules. The whole point is he's this mysterious guy, waiting in the wings for me to unmask him. And he thinks I'm this amazing brainiac who can figure it out."

"Then the poor guy has my sympathy," shouts Teddy from the kitchen. "He's obviously a crazy person."

"Great pep talk, thank you."

I wait for further mockery, but all I get is the whine of the hand mixer, cranked up to the highest setting.

Betsy winces as it makes that awful scrapy sound against the side of the bowl.

"Teddybaby, we don't need pancakes that bad!" she yells, till the whizzing and the scraping stops.

I might need pancakes. She's giving me that "let me explain your own lunacy to you" face.

"Wait up, honeybee, I need to get this straight. There are two guys: this Eric guy you thought was all pretty and kissable, and this Mystery guy who writes you saying he thinks *you're* all pretty and kissable. And when you thought they were the same person, that was all roses, but now they aren't . . . did pretty and kissable Eric suddenly get hideous and disgusting?"

I try to ignore the way Teddy's curls are peeping out from the kitchen doorway, as if the opportunity to smirk is just too tempting, and picture Eric in my head. Eric with his long swishy coat, and his boots, and his eyelashes.

The coat is actually sort of ridiculous and smells like wet dog when it rains. His fingers are yellow. Ludo says he picks his nose. Even the eyelashes do their cheek-sweeping thing a bit too perfectly on cue to be accidental.

I think I liked the *theory* of Peroxide Eric — a studly bad-boy boyfriend — and sort of forgot there was an actual person involved. Several people, in fact. The willing-to-cheat-on-his-girlfriend thing turns out not to be so sexy after all.

"It's . . . complicated. But he's irrelevant anyway. He's one hundred percent disinterested in me."

"U-*huh*. But does that mean you just stop liking him, snap?"

I shrug. Apparently, it kind of does. Unless I'm doing it wrong.

I could be doing it wrong.

"What I'm getting at is . . . you don't have to just say yes to the first guy who says he's interested. You're supposed to choose a boyfriend because you like him, too, you know? Not because he's the only one who asked."

"I *do* like him. I mean, I liked him when I thought he was the guy sending me the e-mails, being all flirty and funny and, just, *getting* me, you know? I get giddy when I see I've got a message from him. I could talk to him for hours. *That guy's the guy I like."*

Unless I'm doing it wrong.

I'm coiling one braid around my finger, thinking about love & affection, while Betsy tries not to crack up. Even Teddy comes out of the kitchen to beam one of his lazy smiles my way.

I'm not doing it wrong.

"All this without even knowing what he looks like? Boy must have some typing skills." She tilts her head, so the bell on her hat gives a little tinkle, then turns serious. "Just be careful, honeybee, OK? Don't want you getting your feelings hurt. Or Mystery Boy's, either."

I nog. I've already had my feelings hurt. I'm practically a veteran at this whole dating thing. And I've got no intention of making the same mistake, and getting distracted by a Mysterious Someone Who Isn't E.

There's another tinkly noise, but this one's from the bell on the Little Leaf door.

It's Simon. Spooky blond not-a-Gothboy Simon, who I keep seeing hanging around the corridors of the Finch, and who still makes me do a double take every time. He gives me a weak smile from under his hair. I give him the same one back again, wondering if he knows about Eric and Fili. Is that what scared all the Goth out of him?

Betsy doesn't look so startled by the transformation, though, as if it's not the first time she's seen it.

"Hey, Simon! What can I get you, honey?"

Simon slides onto the stool next to mine and taps a finger on the counter, thinking.

"Banana bread?" he says, hopefully.

Betsy sucks in a breath, swinging her earrings as she shakes her head.

"Heidi doesn't believe in banana in cake," Teddy explains. "It's like her religion."

This is true. Bananas in fruit form are perfectly acceptable. In cake they result in mushiness, and a lingering aftertaste of yuck. They are the anti-peanut butter: guaranteed to de-yummify anything.

Simon gives me an apologetic look through his wispy hair as Teddy brings him a foul-smelling slice anyway, and fishes in his pocket.

"Maybe take out the order for the Banana Blondies then?" Simon says, sliding an envelope across the counter to Betsy.

She grins as she takes it. "You're the boss. But don't blame me if all those Finch parents start complaining." She catches my blank look, and waves the envelope at me. "You didn't know? It's going to be the Little Leaf's last hurrah: catering for your big musical extravaganza. Guess those rehearsal cupcakes went down pretty good, huh?"

I stare at Simon, as he prods the edge of his banana bread with a fork.

"You organized this? Wow, Simon, that's really . . ."

I want to say unexpected, but it seems kind of rude.

"Are these the new designs?" he says softly, reaching across me to pick up a rolled-up sheaf of paper.

Teddy must have slipped it there next to me, along with the banana bread.

The designs for Etienne and the Illyrians are just as detailed as the last lot: same swooping style for hands and faces, same little handwritten notes and scribbles of color. No ribbons or silver flashes this time, though: it's all skinny gray Lycra bodysuits with bright neon piping, in odd geometric squiggles like the inside of circuits.

"Cool," murmurs Simon, his finger tracing around the neon pink lines.

"It's all based on this film, *Tron*?" I explain. "These people get trapped inside a computer game, and they have to ride bikes and play frisbee to save the universe. It's . . . less ridiculous than that sounds."

"Though not by a whole lot," says Teddy, reappearing to prop himself on his elbows behind the counter.

I catch his eye, and mouth a quick "thank you." He grins, then gives Simon a sideways look, his eyes following Simon's fingertip.

Simon did that before, I remember, with Fili's costume picture. I remember thinking how romantic it seemed. Only now he's doing it to Etienne Gracey's costume, which is . . . also unexpected.

Is there some other non-Eric-shaped reason for Simon and Fili breaking up when they did? Like, Simon suddenly recognizing his inner gay?

He forks in another minute mouthful of banana cake, and gives me another of those watery, apologetic smiles.

WEIGH.

TUP.

Maybe it's not the person whose going to be wearing the costume he likes.

Maybe it's the person who drew the costume. Or the person who he *thinks* drew it anyway.

Simon, who quietly arranges for the Little Leaf to come to *Twelfth Night*.

Simon, who broke up with Fili the exact same night that Mysterious E first e-mailed.

Simon, the reformed Gothboy, who seems used to walking around in disguise.

Simon, aka Mysterious E?

UM.

WOO?

The penthouse. Mycroft Christie is wearing a fluffy blond wig and eating a stinky banana cake.

MYCROFT CHRISTIE: What? You don't like my makeover?

HEIDI: Downgrade. Sorry.

MYCROFT CHRISTIE: (tossing the wig aside and revealing his curls) I confess I agree. But still, one mustn't judge by appearances.

HEIDI: You mean, I'm fugly and a weirdo and I should take what I can get?

MYCROFT CHRISTIE: On the contrary: Mysterious E's

appeal is not too dissimilar to my own, surely? Granted, this "Simon" person lacks certain of my debonair charms, but I fancy my intellect alone makes me quite the catch.

HEIDI: You also fight crime, can travel in time, and have saved the city of London from evil giant centipedes. Even if that episode was a bit crap. And you haven't recently broken up with one of my mates, who is already really miserable, for complicated reasons that I probably can't even tell you about.

MYCROFT CHRISTIE: You do have intimidatingly high standards for your gentleman friends, Miss Ryder. Besides, I believe your intention — this time — was to ascertain the identity of your mysterious suitor before any awkward encounters on sofas could ensue. Might I propose a little further investigation?

Agent Ryder is starting to feel overwhelmed by the pressures of undercover life at the Finch. Pre-Christmas cheer is beginning to creep throughout the school, thanks mostly to Dad Man being bored and Wassail decorations being harder to find: tinsel around the notice boards, a tree as tall as the Manor on the front steps that's speckled with white and blue lights. But behind all the fake snow and baubles in every classroom, every corridor, there seems to be a lurking secret, a little subtext, a dangerous casual slip that could bring it all tumbling down.

Eric loiters outside the music rooms while PAG rehearsals go on, waiting for Scheherezade to come out, while Ludo watches him from inside, her chin firmly up as she twirls to show what he's missing. Fili watches Ludo twirl, her face downcast, till she sees me looking and ducks her head, while I remember that even Ed doesn't know why she might be looking so guilty, and turn away, to find Dai, watching me closely, just as Ed asked him to, while Henry lingers off to one side, waiting for him to move on so he can slide in and share some not-a-birthday-or-a-party ideas.

The only person I never seem to bump into is Simon — though that must mean something.

I'm a little bit relieved (though I wouldn't even tell Mycroft Christie that).

But I can't avoid Simon when Venables calls a grand PAG meeting in the auditorium, with compulsory attendance for all.

"Brilliant, brilliant, come in, do!" he yelps, hair flapping as he beckons us in from the cold.

The auditorium has got its festive party mojo going, too. All the tiered seats have been pulled out and pushed forward, taking over what was empty rehearsal space and throwing all attention toward the stage, where giant plywood stiletto heels and cocktail glasses are stacking up. There are inflatable flamingos dangling from the lighting rig. Tucked away in the wings are rows of metal wardrobe frames, where I can see some of the finished costumes hanging up: silver flashes mixing with ribbons and epaulettes.

We climb into the weirdly bouncy seats, precariously raised up above the stage, and I somehow end up sitting between Henry and Simon. Henry whispers rapidly into my ear about his brilliant idea for an Unparty for Dai's Unbirthday, while Simon says nothing — just stares mistily into the distance through his hair in a way he probably thinks is enigmatic and sort of sexy.

I can see Dai watching me keenly, an "I thought so" look on his face.

OPE.

OO.

He thinks it's Simon, too.

I try to catch Ludo's eye, but she seems to be ducking mine suddenly.

I don't want to look at Fili, a few rows below: It's all too awkward.

"So, guys, guys, thank you for coming!" says Venables, skipping a bit with excitement. "Now, I know you've been working hard, I know you're all tired, so I thought it was time you had a little break, and a little treat."

There's a chorus of oohing. Apparently no one else is as worried as me about what Venables's idea of a treat might be.

"So this weekend, we're going to fly away from the Goldfinch nest and see how the professionals do it. Not a musical version, no, but after Mr. Prowse expressed a few, uh, *concerns*, Mrs. Kemble is very keen to emphasize the educational aspect of this year's performance to your parents. So we'll be heading to the theatre, to see *Twelfth Night*, the original William Shakespeare, no help from me, version. Brilliant, yeah?"

There's no oohing.

"And of course, it'll be a late night, so we'll be staying over in Stratford and coming back by bus the next day."

Now there's oohing. And shrieking, and even, from one corner, a round of applause.

Not from me, though.

I should be thrilled. This won't be just like any other school trip I've been on before. Usually I'm the kid who has to share a seat on the bus with the teacher, because she's the Mothership, or just because I don't have any friends. This time, I'll have someone to insist I share with them — and someone to keep my seat in the theatre, someone to sneak out of bed for once the teachers have gone to sleep, just like a real Finch: like a real girl, with a real boyfriend. I'll be on the trip with my Mysterious E. I just wish he weren't Simon, that's all.

Venables is still beaming and waving his arms in front of us, flapping some papers to get us to quiet down.

"That's not all, folks, there's more good news! Now, I know everyone in this room is super-talented in their own way, and you know I'm proud of you all, yeah? But a lot of your work goes on behind the scenes, and on the big night it's all about the performers, so I'm totally thrilled to have a chance to big up one of the real stars of the show. You've all seen our amazing costumes, yeah?"

There are murmurs of approval in the crowd as Venables flings an arm to the wardrobe racks at the edge of the stage. He grabs a curled pile of papers and waves them over his head. Teddy's designs. I start to feel a bit sick.

"Well, I was so impressed with the work that went into these, I showed them to Mr. Bowser in the art department, and *he* was so impressed that he's entered the artist into the Independent Schools National Arts Prize. Heidi? Heidi, give us a wave, yeah? Brilliant."

Henry grabs my arm, and waggles it about, as people clap and cheer.

EEK.

ARG.

UR.

There's a blur of people moving round me, climbing over the rows of seats, telling me how amazing I am. Even Etienne Gracey leans over to give me a quick pat on the back.

I manage to get onto my feet, and start edging my way along the row, mumbling apologies as I push past the slow-moving people on the steps down to ground level. I have to tell Venables I didn't draw those costumes. It'll be awful and horrible and everyone will hate me, but I can't let them put me up for some daft art prize. I have to tell the truth.

I let the crowd sweep me out through the doors into the foyer, then duck through Music Room 1, find the backstage steps, and hurry up into the wings. Venables is at the front of the stage, kneeling down, and muttering something about spotlights to Oliver Bass.

I hesitate, waiting for him to stand, then I force my feet, one in front of the other, to move me forward, out onto the stage. It feels strange, seeing the seats all rising up out of the dark out there, all facing my way.

My feet keep on stepping, but someone has my arm, and is pulling me back. Dai. Dai, with a face like thunder.

"I don't know what you think you're doing, Ryder, but you can knock it off right now, yeah?"

I blink. Does Dai know that Teddy drew the pictures? Does Dai *care* that Teddy drew the pictures?

"You two might think you're being dead clever," he says, yanking me into the wings, behind the guilt-inducing racks of costumes. "But I'm not blind. I do see things. Especially if you carry on with it right under my nose."

Not the pictures, then. Simon. He's angry with me about Simon. I think.

"Why do you care?" I stutter, looking round and hoping no one else is listening. I'm having a fight over a boyfriend I don't even want. Does *Dai* want to go out with Simon, then?

Dai goes from looking furious to looking like a kicked puppy in the blink of an eye. His big shoulders drop. I think for an awful moment that he might actually cry.

"I really like him, Heidi. He's the first person I've ever really liked, who really liked me back. At least, I thought he did. But then I started watching you, because . . . well, never mind why, I just knew you were looking for someone else after you'd broken up with Ed, and then suddenly you two were sneaking off together to talk, and he started being all secretive, and . . ."

"Wait. You think . . . me and *Henry* . . . ?"

And I thought I was the hopeless detective around here.

"Well, why else would you be going off for your secret get-togethers?"

My mouth opens. I close it again. No, there's nothing for it: I'm going to have to spoil Henry's secret birthday plans.

But Dai doesn't wait to hear the truth: He just sticks up his chin and stomps off down the backstage steps, pushing Ludo out of his way as he goes.

She stares after him, hesitating at the bottom of the stairs, then hurries up them to me.

"OH MY GOD, what is HIS problem?"

I just shake my head. Explaining is a bit beyond me right now.

Ludo hovers, gazing up at the lighting rig above, the invisible audience beyond, her eyes shiny. Her painted fingers walk along the row of hanging costumes, toying with the dangling ribbons.

"OK, like, this is probably a totally weird question," she says, looking strangely shy. "But, like, I just wanted to check that it would be OK with you first, because . . . well . . . you've got a new boyfriend now, right?"

"Um . . . kind of?"

"I totally thought so. Which is, like, yay Heidi! So, you know, you won't be getting back together with Ed?"

The sick feeling comes back.

"Because, if you aren't going out with him, then I thought maybe I might go out with him? Actually, we're sort of going out already. Or, you know, talking about it. Kind of?" She flips her glossy hair back and gives me a nervous little smile. "He's really sweet, isn't he?"

"Yeah," I mumble. "He's . . . um . . ."

"I'm so happy!" she says, wrapping her arms round my neck. "Because I totally wouldn't if it wasn't OK with you, and I would totally understand if it wasn't, because, you know, friends don't do that to each other. But if you're OK with it, then everything's, like, totally perfect!"

And she goes pirouetting off down the steps, leaping over the last couple in full view of a loitering Peroxide Eric, with a look of gleeful don't-care upon her face.

Evasive maneuvers, Captain. Abort, abort! Engage the hyperdrive immediately.

I peer out from behind the sleeve of Viola's blue jacket, looking for an escape route. Venables blocks my way, holding up Teddy's sketches for the band, showing off the details to Etienne, and the Illyrians, and . . . the Mothership.

I retreat backward, into the scratchy silvery safety of the Niteclubbers clothes rail, enveloping me like some kind of spandex route to Narnia. I can't do this now. I'll fix it later. I promise I'll come back and sort it all out, when my head isn't spinning around with all the craziness of Dai and Henry, and Ludo and Ed, and Simon.

Simon, who I can see heading directly for the clothes rail, right toward where I'm hiding.

Simon, smiling his watery smile.

Simon, who's holding hands with Yuliya, wispy silent blond Yuliya, who is smiling, too.

They giggle as they slide between the two rails of clothes, sneaking out of sight of the crowd. I feel the clothes sweep over my head as they pass; see their shoes interlock; hear more giggling, following by snoggy noises.

I should be relieved. Mysterious E isn't Simon.

But I'm not sure it matters. I've messed everything up. Gingerbread Ed, and E. D. Hartley, and the Leftover Squad: It's all gone too far. I don't belong here, with them. I'll never belong here.

Message from: gingerbread_ed <gingerbread_ed@frogmail.com>
Subject: good-bye

hey,

i'm going away on an exchange trip to peru where i hear they don't have the internet probably. so i guess i won't be around much because it is a very long exchange trip. sorry about everything.

ed

to: bloodwinetears@letterbox.com
from: gingerbread_ed@frogmail.com

dear fili,

i'm sorry, but i think i have to stop writing to you. i can't really explain properly, and i really hope you know you have other people around you who would love to be able to talk with you like the old days. but with me and heidi not being together and everything, now seems like the right time to call this a day.

ed

to: gingerbread_ed@frogmail.com
from: bloodwinetears@letterbox.com

Dear Ed,

It's perfect timing. I'm leaving, you see. Flying the nest. Escaping from it all, the very next time they open the cage. Running away, to where they'll never find me.

Fili

Recipe for The End of the World

INGREDIENTS:

No friends
No life
No hope

METHOD:

- It is too late.
- There is no method.
- Just stand back as everything falls apart.

○ ○

An attic. Ridiculous fictional detective Mycroft Christie is inexplicably present, talking to the unfortunately not-imaginary Miss Heidi Ryder.

HEIDI: I don't know what to do.

MYCROFT CHRISTIE: Nonsense! There's always a Plan B.

HEIDI: Yes. And a Plan C, and a Plan D, and Plan Z, and all of them will be stupid, like making up people who don't exist, and handcuffs, and thinking I'm a detective when I'm too stupid to notice anything at all, and all of it is no use anyway because there's actual real proper difficult life stuff happening to actual real people. I don't need a Plan. I need to help my friend Fili. Go away, please?

MYCROFT CHRISTIE: I'm afraid I can't. I'm your subconscious mind's default response whenever faced with a crisis.

HEIDI: Can you *fix* the crisis?

MYCROFT CHRISTIE: I can defuse nuclear weapons with a fountain pen?

HEIDI: Nice. Can you help Fili?

MYCROFT CHRISTIE: (smoldery eyebrow, seductive nostril flare, manly yet vulnerable teardrop on brink of falling)

HEIDI: That's really helpful, thanks.

MYCROFT CHRISTIE: At least I'm here for you to talk to. After all, you aren't exactly blessed with potential alternatives. Betsy is somewhat preoccupied with moving. The Mothership would have to involve the school: perhaps not the most diplomatic choice? And as for friends . . . Young Dai seems to be under the impression you're rather devious: I doubt he'll want to listen. Dear Ludo is unfortunately besotted with . . . well, *you*, not that she knows that: more than a little awkward. Then there's Simon, who doesn't love you after all: how tragic, to be disappointed about someone you never even wanted. I imagine he's rather busy with his new girlfriend anyway. . . .

HEIDI: It's not them I want to talk to anyway. It's Fili.

MYCROFT CHRISTIE: But Miss Heidi Ryder knows nothing. Fili didn't choose to tell her: She told dear, kind, sensitive Ed.

HEIDI: It doesn't matter. If people find out about Ed, it doesn't matter, not now. I don't care.

MYCROFT CHRISTIE: Don't you think Fili might care? Don't you think Fili might be even more hurt, to learn the one person she thought she could trust was nothing but cinnamon and dust?

HEIDI: So what am I supposed to do?

MYCROFT CHRISTIE: Don't ask me. I don't exist.

to: bloodwinetears@letterbox.com
from: gingerbread_ed@frogmail.com

dear fili,

are you serious? where would you go? please don't do anything drastic right now.

ed

to: bloodwinetears@letterbox.com
from: gingerbread_edfrogmail.com

dear fili,

i don't know what to do. do you want me to tell someone about this? do you want me to help?

ed

to: bloodwinetears@letterbox.com
from: gingerbread_ed@frogmail.com

dear fili,

i wish you'd talk to me.

ed

to: heidi.ryder@goldfinch.ac.uk
from: arealboy@letterbox.com

Dearest Heidi,

Patient as I am, I find myself feeling dreadfully neglected of late, and contrary to popular song we do not have all the time in the world. Might I beg for a fragment of your kind attention? Or should I fear your attentions are truly swayed in the direction of another?

Rest assured, you continue to have my

love & affection,
E

to: arealboy@letterbox.com
from: heidi.ryder@goldfinch.ac.uk

Dear E,

Look, now is really not a good time for all this stupid messing about pretending to talk funny, all right? Some of us have more important things to worry about.

Just forget about me, please? Because, whoever you are, I'm really not worth it, and I totally don't have time for this.

Heidi

to: heidi.ryder@goldfinch.ac.uk
from: arealboy@letterbox.com

Dearest Heidi,

How terribly intriguing you are determined to be. But please, leave the noble sacrifices to the gentleman of the party? I can't play my part if you steal all my best lines, after all.

As ever, I am at your service.

love & affection,
E

(P.S. Seriously, you OK? I can't ever tell when you're kidding.)

"If you don't want to go on the theatre trip, babes, you don't have to."

The Mothership stares anxiously at my untouched plate of mashed up butternut squash and pumpkin seeds, which I probably wouldn't have wanted even if it didn't feel like I have a canoe in my throat.

But I shake my head, and tell her I want to go. Fili has been skipping classes. Yuliya's been telling everyone Fili's got a cold, but I bet she'll be well enough to come on the bus. I'm just scared she's not planning to come back.

Which is how I end up on my way to watch a comedy about cross-dressing shipwrecked twins when reality is roller coastering its way off a cliff: not in space, not in a pirate ship, not with any monkeys or explosions or leather trousers. Just an ordinary cliff, with ordinarily hard, pointy rocks at the bottom.

I try to sit next to Fili on the bus, but Ludo spotwelds herself to my elbow and talks Ed all the way there.

I try to snag a shared room with her in the hostel they've booked for the overnight stay, but Prowse has allocated the rooms, and Fili's down the other end of the hall.

I try to sit next to her in the theatre, but Henry grabs my arm and forces me to sit between him and Dai, to Dai's obvious irritation. I shoot out of my seat between acts to see if I can sit next to Fili for the rest of the play.

But she's not in the bar, not in the toilets, not in the theatre at all.

I can hear Venables yelling after me as I sprint down the stairs, but I'm not stopping for him, or anyone. I run back the five-minute walk back to the hostel, heart pounding. We're in funny little dorms in an annex round the back of a hostel, the kind that knows what teenagers smell like and doesn't want us to puke on the proper paying customers over their bacon and eggs in the morning. Girls on one floor, boys on the other, two bunks to a room. I hurry past the room I'm sharing with Ludo, past all the others, hoping I've remembered the number right. Hoping I'm not too late.

Fili's at the other end of the hallway, sharing with Yuliya. Room number 13. An omen. Just has to be.

I hammer on the door.

Silence.

I hammer again, dropping my hands to rest on my knees, resting my head against the door to catch my breath. Then there's a click, and I'm falling forward, knocking her back onto the lower bunk.

She's still here.

She's still here.

She looks cold and sort of angry. Fully dressed, eyelinered, boots on.

Her suitcase is on the floor by her feet, zipped up, waiting.

"Aren't you missing the play?" she says, quietly.

I get this spooky little flash of us, together, perched on the end of the balance beam for the first time all those months ago. All I'd known about Fili before that was her amazing ability to say Go Away, loud and clear, with just a flick of her eyebrow. And suddenly there she'd been, swinging her boots and sharing her music: a friend for the Frog Girl. She wasn't just this little black cloud, anymore than I was just this faculty brat. She was dark and funny and interesting and odd, and the only time I saw the Go Away look was when she was defending one of us from some Finch meathead.

I'm getting the Go Away look now.

It hurts, but I've probably earned it.

Fili lifts a hand up and rests it on the top of her case. She drums her fingers as if she's waiting for me to leave. I nearly do. But that's not what I came here for.

"Look, just . . . don't run away, yeah? I mean, if you were thinking of it."

She rolls her eyes, unzips the suitcase, and lets it fall open. It's empty.

"Oh. So . . . you're not running away then?"

She shakes her head, slowly.

"Oh. Well, good. I thought you . . . I mean, Ed thought . . ."

She flips the suitcase lid down again, and looks at me sadly.

OH.

OH.

Something in my head clicks into place.

"You know, don't you?" I say, my voice coming out all thick. "About Ed. I mean, you know he's . . ." I swallow. It feels so odd, saying it out loud. "He's not real. He never was real. I just . . . made him up."

Fili nods, just once.

I flop down on the bunk bed, next to her. "I always did think he was kind of obvious. Poetic boy with motorbike who no one can ever meet who happens to fall madly in love with me? I didn't really expect anyone to believe in him."

"You just put him on the internet by accident. And then wrote all those messages. By accident."

I feel my toes knotting together, and I hang my head. It's probably a good thing we're sitting side by side. Makes it easier not to see her face.

"It just kind of got out of hand, honest. Dai and Ludo started talking to him, and it seemed like it couldn't hurt anyone, you know?"

"It hurt me," she says.

OW.

"Think I was jealous," she says, with a tiny sad smile.

242

"But I was jealous of you! You had Simon, and you seemed like you were so happy, and always together. And you never talked to Ed like the others did, though I suppose I get why now. I thought you didn't like me anymore."

"I thought the same thing about you," she says, slowly. "I wanted to talk to you. Not Ed-you, Heidi-you. I wanted to tell you how unhappy I was with Simon, how crowded I felt, the way he was always following me around, copying me. How I felt about . . ."

I look up as she cuts herself off, and shakes her head.

"I don't know why I'm angry with you," she sighs. "It's me who screwed up. I sort of had a thing with Eric. While he was still going out with Ludo."

I squirm on the bed. "I know. I mean, I figured it out. Eventually."

"I've wondered if you knew for ages," she says, sounding almost relieved. "The way you kept staring at him like you knew something wasn't right."

I squirm a bit more.

She sighs, and twines her fingers in the tassels of her scarf, looking impossibly sad.

"You want to know what hurt me the most, though?" she says, not looking up.

I look at my feet. I don't even know what the worst of it is: There are way too many contenders for the prize.

"The worst of it is . . . you actually believed all that emo crap I wrote."

HUH?

A wan smile tugs at her lips.

"I don't send complete strangers e-mails about my rainbows of despair, Heidi. 'The garden of love is a thorny threshold'? I'm offended. When I do pain, I do it better than that. I kept expecting you to call me on it, but, well, apparently that's what I am to you: the sad clown, with tears on her face."

"I didn't draw that," I blurt out.

She raises an eyebrow. Drops it again. Comes up with a totally unexpected rueful laugh. I haven't seen her do that in . . . I'm not sure I've ever seen her do that.

"We really are the screw-up twins," she sighs, all the coldness gone from her voice now.

"So . . . you were just messing around? All that stuff about being unhappy, that was just . . . for entertainment? To punish me?"

The smile dies away, and she shrugs. "Well, some of it."

I think I know what she means. Half-play-acting, half-truth: I know that game pretty well.

I've been the worst friend imaginable. I thought I must be lonely, to have to make up a Gingerbread Ed, but Fili *only* had him to talk to. No Ludo because of Eric; no Simon, who wasn't the perfect boyfriend at all; no Betsy; no Mycroft Christie; not even a Mothership. And no me, because I was off with my precious Ed.

"I'm so sorry, Fili."

She shrugs. "Team effort. Don't think either of us was thinking all that straight. I do get why you kept Ed around, you know. It was fun for a while, pretending to be someone else: talking up all my problems, waiting for it to sound bad enough for you — the real you — to step in. Only you wouldn't do it. You kept my secret, *all* my secrets, to stop anyone from finding out yours. All to protect a boy who doesn't exist."

She stops and sighs, as if using up an entire month's word quota in one go has worn her out a bit. As if she might change her mind and go back to hating me.

There are totally other reasons, I want to say: other really good reasons, like me thinking Ed could help her more than useless, thoughtless Heidi, and all those times I wanted to say something, and how I thought she'd never forgive me if I did tell, and how much I *missed* her, but then the Eric thing got so confusing, and Simon, and Mysterious E, and . . .

WOE.

UH.

I can hardly get the words out.

"Fili . . . are *you* E? Are you A Real Boy?"

She blinks at me. "No idea what you're talking about. Things are definitely back to normal."

They aren't, I know, not really. It'll take a little while for that. But she smiles, and I remember what I've been trying to do forever, and give her a hug. She hugs me back. It's the best feeling in the world.

"You can tell the others," I say, kicking at the ugly pink carpet. "Or I'll tell them. About Ed, I mean. If you want. They'll never speak to me again, probably, but I kind of deserve that."

Fili frowns. "Are you going to tell Ludo about Eric and me?"

"No," I say, without hesitating. "They're over now. They were already over. She's better off without him anyway. It'd only hurt her feelings."

"So how about you keep my secret, and I'll keep yours?"

Can it be that easy? Is this a test?

"I'll delete him completely," I say, in a rush. "I won't write any more messages from Ed, to anyone. Just total and complete honesty from now on, I promise."

She nods, then frowns.

"What was that about A Real Boy?"

I blush, and fiddle with the end of my left braid, and start to explain.

Heidi and Fili, hanging out and talking about boys, like best friends do.

Recipe for a Brand-new Heidi

INGREDIENTS:

An old, slightly worn Heidi
Friends
Honesty
The musical stylings of Kajagoogoo

METHOD:

• Take care to remove all traces of gingerbread, detectives, and boys (imaginary or otherwise) from your Heidi.
• Soak her in tea and company for two weeks.
• Unwrap her like a Christmas present.

○ ○ ○ ○ ○ ○ ○ ○ ○ ○ ○ ○ ○ ○ ○ ○ ○ ○ ○ ○

A dimly lit penthouse, which looks uncannily like a small, untidy attic bedroom belonging to a fifteen-year-old girl. Mycroft Christie, time-traveling private investigator, is sulking, while Miss Heidi Ryder stares him down.

MYCROFT CHRISTIE: This is absolutely . . .

HEIDI: (holding up a finger sharply) Oi!

MYCROFT CHRISTIE: But I'm merely . . .

HEIDI: Final warning!

MYCROFT CHRISTIE: My dear girl, this is quite — I say, why am I walking into the wardrobe? And closing the door? And putting this pair of socks into my mouth?

HEIDI: I'm sure a detective genius like you will figure it out.

MYCROFT CHRISTIE: *Mmffwwwwhhfff.*

HEIDI: Couldn't have put it better myself.

"I knew there was a reason I was single," sighs Betsy, perching on one of the only chairs left in the strangely naked-looking Little Leaf.

"Trust me, I'm staying that way," I tell her, dunking my chocolate chip cookie a bit fiercely into my tea. "No more boy action for Heidi. Not that I've had any boy action. But if any comes my way, I'm sending it right back to the manufacturer."

"Oh, it's going to come your way, honey. You're quite the magnet. Straight girls, gay guys . . ."

"Have I mentioned lately how much I'm *not* going to miss you? Anyway, it was *Ed* who attracted Ludo, which is completely not the same thing. And I only attracted Henry inside Dai's crazy brain, which is all sorted out now, thank you."

"What about your mystery guy?"

"Mysterious E? Out of the picture."

"Oh, you figured out who that was then?" asks Teddy, shunting cardboard boxes across the floor with his foot.

"Nope. But I don't care. *No more boy action for Heidi.*" I tink my spoon against my mug with each word, just to drill it in.

Teddy blinks, gives me a slightly perturbed look (which is probably fair enough — he doesn't really need to know about my boy action), and escapes out of the door with his boxes.

"It's probably for the best, hon. I mean, don't take this the wrong way, but he does kind of fit your pattern."

"My pattern? I have a pattern?"

Betsy dips her chin, so she can peer at me over the top of some invisible glasses.

"OK, let's run through the selection of boys that seem to have been taking up all your energy lately. First up: Ed. Charming and all, but just a little bit on the imaginary side. Then we have the Mysterious E contenders, right? Which would be . . ."

"Eric."

"Dating one of your best friends."

Dating two, it turns out, in fact, though I'm pretty sure that's not going to help my case exactly.

"Then Simon."

"Dating another one of your best friends."

Also dating someone else, though I'm pretty sure there wasn't an overlap.

"Then Henry. Though *I* never thought that! All in Dai's hyperactive imagination."

"But he is . . . ?"

"Dating one of my best friends." It still feels a little odd saying "best friends" like that. I was pretty sure I wouldn't have any a week ago. But you can fit a lot of apologizing and "Can we just forget that ever happened?" into a week. I might still have a shot at belonging, after all.

I sulk into my tea, feeling guilty again.

"Yep, OK, I get it. I'm a big shameless boy-stealing ho. In my imagination, at least."

Betsy takes the mug away, so I can't lurk behind it anymore.

"No, honeypie, that's not it. The pattern's not that they're people your friends are dating. The pattern is that they're unavailable. Which makes them . . . safe. Like your gingerbread man. A boy can't hurt you if you make him up. And he can't break your heart if you'll never, ever get to date him."

"But that doesn't make him *safe*. That makes him . . . suck-tastic. Not to mention a buttload of work. I've done the imaginary boyfriend thing: Seriously, that is not a relaxing gig. I mean, not that it matters now anyway, but Mysterious E's not the same deal at all."

"Really? So what is it you like about him? His taste in music? The color of his eyes? His laugh, his walk, that cute little thing he does when no one's looking? Or do you like that he doesn't have any of those things, so you can make them up yourself?"

I take my mug back, and frown into it.

"You can't control everything, hon," she says.

to: arealboy@letterbox.com
from: heidi.ryder@goldfinch.ac.uk

Dearest E,

Apparently I only ever liked you because you're a figment of my imagination. Or something. So this is good-bye.

H

to: heidi.ryder@goldfinch.ac.uk
from: arealboy@letterbox.com

Dearest Heidi,

How unfortunate: I was rather looking forward to my grand unveiling. I thought a certain forthcoming end-of-term event might be a suitably dramatic occasion?

Wouldn't you like me to prove my non-figment nature once and for all?

love & affection,

E

to: arealboy@letterbox.com
from: heidi.ryder@goldfinch.ac.uk

Dearest E,

No!

H

to: heidi.ryder@goldfinch.ac.uk
from: arealboy@letterbox.com

Dearest Heidi,

I'm not at all sure I'll be able to carry out your wishes on this subject, my dear. We figments are rather stubborn that way.

You could always prove your utter disinterest by failing to reply?

love & affection,
E

to: arealboy@letterbox.com
from: heidi.ryder@goldfinch.ac.uk

Dearest E,

Honestly, I'm really not going out with people at the moment, so you really shouldn't bother trying all this stuff.

H

to: heidi.ryder@goldfinch.ac.uk
from: arealboy@letterbox.com

Dearest Heidi,

Thank you. :)

love & affection,
E

The Finch is winding down for the end of term. The teachers have given up pretending to actually teach us anything, and lessons are now just finishing off bits of coursework, or falling asleep in the corner because you already have. The kitchen staff is all humming Christmas carols with a little '80s twist, thanks to the daily PAG rehearsals. I've even handed in a Poem on an Autumn Leaf to Prowse's satisfaction.

It's not all relaxation for me, though. As part of my newly reformed truth-telling mission (Ludo quietly excluded, so I don't have to break her heart), I've confessed I wasn't the one who drew the costume designs to Venables. Cue my first ever personal audience with Mrs. Kemble, who is inconveniently not the Demon Headmistress after all (glowy red eyes, little horns hiding under her perm, mockable pointy tail) but the sort of person who says awkward things about me letting down my mum and dad, who aren't very mockable at all. The Mothership and Dad Man have tried quite hard to blame the negative influence of Finches, but I'm trying to cure them of that. I feel so guilty about this whole term, it's actually kind of a relief to be properly in trouble.

Plus my punishment is pretty entertaining. I'm on litter-picking duty every break time as penance. I get to walk around the gardens dressed like a plasticated beekeeper, with a big prongy thing and a plastic bag, which happens to be the ideal outfit for Dai's birthday.

I do hesitate before heading over to the Lake common room, wondering if I really will be welcome. But I'm curious to know how an Unbirthday Unparty works, beyond the invitation's demand to "Dress Unfestively." And Henry doesn't disappoint.

The common room has been Unimpressively Undecorated. There are popped balloons in multiple colors, flat limp blobs dangling pathetically off string. There's a banner strung up along the wall above the TV (playing Brazil on mute), with the words HAPPY BIRTHDAY masked out in black paint. On the coffee table sit jelly molds shaped like rabbits, all empty: A silver foil square of card has been speared with a single birthday candle, as if the cake in between the two suddenly vanished. And presiding over all is Henry, dressed in black, wearing a cone-shaped party hat (painted black, right down to the streamers), swaying gently to some epically miserable cello music.

I've never been to a funeral, but I'm guessing this is pretty close. It's horrible. It's kind of tasteless. Dai's going to love it.

We do the obligatory hiding-behind-the-sofa-SURPRISE! bit. Dai does the obligatory I've-no-idea-you're-behind-the-sofa-I'M-SURPRISED! bit in return. Most of the Lower School PAG crowd turn up, all making the effort, suitably dressed down. It's as if, just for Dai, half the school's gone Novelty Goth — except for Scheherezade, who sticks out in her sparkly gold dress like tinsel in spring, and Fili, who has done her best to break with form, and is wearing a bright pink scarf of Ludo's on top of the usual uniform.

And then there's me, in my billowy plastic boiler suit, which turns out to be a bit sweaty when worn indoors.

"You've excelled yourself," says Dai, grabbing the prongy thing and trying to pick up a plastic cup (filled with only water, naturally) with its pincers.

"Truly, the least birthday partyish outfit I've ever witnessed," says Henry. "And waterproof, too!" he adds, as Dai's prongy skills fail him.

I grin. "It's also sprayed with an antibacterial formula, which smells a bit like fish. Don't hug me."

They shrink back, and wander off to prong Scheherezade in the head, though Dai sneaks back later and gives me a hug anyway.

"Best birthday ever," he whispers, yanking on a braid.

I grin, stupidly. I might nearly have it messed up. I might never be able to tell him the truth about Ed, but at least I helped Henry get this right.

Ludo flumps down next to me in an armchair later, still somehow looking gorgeous, even wearing baggy pajamas with her hair dragged into a scraggly topknot. I still need to make all this up to her, somehow. I still see her pop up in UChat every now and then, looking for Ed, always hopeful that he might return from Peru.

I get a little ghost of an old idea. Just a gesture, like an early Christmas present. A really, really good, one-time-only, remember-this-forever Christmas present.

She leans over, tugging my plasticky arm.

"Oh my God, can you BELIEVE Dai thought you and Henry were, like, a thing?"

I look over to the two of them, mock-slow-dancing to the cellos in the middle of the room. Dai's ears are bright red, his cheeks glowing in pink patches, as if even he's just the tiniest bit self-conscious under all this attention. Henry's laughing, his hair sticking out under the elastic of the party hat, as if he knows exactly what Dai's thinking, as if he's proud of making it happen.

I can believe it, sort of. Because inside Dai's head he doesn't deserve all this: not wilted balloons, not invisible cakes, not a boyfriend at all, let alone this one.

And I think:

OH.

That's what I haven't got. I don't mean Henry. I don't even mean the slow dance with someone's hands at my hips, the silly whispered in-jokes, the eye lock as foreheads touch, then noses, then lips. Those I can invent: those I *have* invented. But I haven't got a boy who'll make me an Unparty while I'm not looking, because even though I say I don't want one, I really do. I haven't got a boy who knows me better than I know myself. And I think I might sort of need one, because I don't think I know me at all.

Fili comes to join us, perching on the arm of the armchair, just as drawn into the slow dance of epic romance going on before us.

"They look so happy," Fili murmurs, slipping her feet under Ludo's legs to keep them warm.

"I know," Ludo sighs, hugging a cushion to her chest. "Oh my God, like, LOOK at us? Three hopeless single girls, staring at the unavailablest boys EVER. We're, like, SO pathetic."

"Who says we're all single?" says Fili, that increasingly familiar smile quirking her lips.

Ludo's mouth opens wide as she looks first at Fili, then at me. Then it opens even wider, as she realizes Fili is nodding my way.

"Nuh-uh!" I say, my plasticlike arms making crinkly noises as I wave my hands. "Don't look at me. I'm not seeing anyone. "

"Not *yet*."

"Oh my God, Heidi! Tell us EVERYTHING. And no being

all secretive like last time! We need details. No, wait. Dai! Henry, stop snogging his face off and get over here!"

I shrink down in my antibacterial balloon, as Fili prompts me through an explanation of the adventures of Mysterious E (minus the extremely awkward bits). I keep expecting them to break out into total mockery at my pathetic attempts at romance, but instead they're full of glee and questions.

"So is he a Finch? He must be a Finch."

"Has he given you any clues?"

"Is he hot?"

"Ludo, she doesn't even know his name. How's she supposed to know if he's hot?"

"She knows his name's E. If that's his real name."

"Whose name begins with an *E*?"

"Dude, it's probably a code name."

"What's the point of that? Doesn't he want her to know who he is?"

"That's all part of the game. You know, working it out?"

I glance up and catch Fili's eye, hoping I can show her how grateful I am. But she's glowing herself, at the easy, silly conversation: at being a part of it all, again, excited just as much as me. We've both missed this.

"Like detectives?"

"I suppose."

"Can we be detectives?" Ludo nudges me with a pointy elbow. "I bet we'd be really good detectives."

"We could have outfits."

"Disguises! We'll go undercover as . . . attentive students."

"We'll track him down for you, Ryder. Mysterious E isn't going to be Mysterious for much longer."

They're all grinning like idiots: Ludo, Dai, Henry, Fili. And me: not Miss Ryder or Mysterious H, but the same old dorky Scrabble-playing braid-headed Heidi. The Leftover Squad is back, embarking on our very first investigation, and I don't even have to make it up.

Agent Ryder resumes her covert surveillance activity, which turns out to be much more fun when it's not quite so covert. After all, it doesn't really matter if we get caught. Dad Man can find Henry and Dai on the Manor stairs, dressed like ninjas, peering through the banisters to monitor the passers-by while I loiter as bait — and he just thinks we're being typically end-of-term weird. The Mothership can wonder why Fili and Ludo actually turn up to cross-country running for the first time all year — and dismiss their determination to run with the boys with the obvious explanation. And if Mysterious E happens to notice I'm being even more dorky than usual — well, he might just have to get used to that.

Trying to fit it all in around the last week of musical rehearsals doesn't get us very far with figuring out who my E could be. It's quite a relief to know I'm not the only rubbish detective around here. But I'm starting to get as nervous as they are, gearing up for the big performance. Giddy with anticipation, mildly terrified, sleepless at night, trying to picture how it'll go — whether I'll mess up my lines, fall over, faint the moment the spotlight hits me.

But I don't need to imagine it. I just have to wait.

to: arealboy@letterbox.com
from: heidi.ryder@goldfinch.ac.uk

Dearest E,

Will you really be at the musical? I mean, how will I know you're you?

H

to: heidi.ryder@goldfinch.ac.uk
from: arealboy@letterbox.com

Dearest Heidi,

A less determined soul might find your continuing bafflement discouraging. Am I really so invisible?

As to the night itself, worry not. I imagine you'll find me easy enough to notice.

Until the day, my enduring

love & affection,

E

And then it's here. The Big Day. The Season Finale. The Grand Unveiling.

It's not all happiness. It's the end of term: Tomorrow it'll be time for awkward farewells in front of parents you'd forgotten these people had, before all the shiny cars roll down the hill. The end of the Little Leaf, too. Saying good-bye to Betsy is going to be like saying good-bye to cake itself. Promising to write and send pictures to cake, being reassured that cake will call every now and then to say hi, knowing that this will only remind you of how you don't have cake anymore and can never have cake again, when it's *cake*, you know? Wondrous cake. (I'm not telling Betsy the cake metaphor. It's possibly misinterpretable.) And who's going to put cookie dough in my hair, and show me ridiculous '80s movies, and not mind a dork like me staring goofily at those beautiful twinkly eyes, and ruffly curls, and that slow lazy smile. . . .

Maybe it's a good thing he's leaving. I've had enough imaginary romance just lately.

I'm barred from helping out with the last-minute setting up in the auditorium, thanks to the costuming embarrassment, so I try to distract myself by heading into town, for one last look at the crazy walls, one last chance to smell the waft of tea and baking. I need to ask Teddy for one last favor, too, for Ludo's extra-special Christmas present, if that isn't pushing my luck. Maybe I can even get a little bit of the inevitable tearful hugging out of the way, before I see them again tonight, up at the Finch. But the door's locked. The walls have already been painted over with grungy white. Even the furniture's gone.

I hope Mysterious E won't mind having a bit of a snotty girlfriend: I'm sniffly already.

He'll hold my hand, though. Lend me a tissue. Sigh fondly at me, the way boyfriends do.

I head home, and waste the afternoon experimenting with the Mothership's waterproof mascara, until she's outside, honking the horn, and suddenly it's all beginning, for real.

The pillared Manor entrance is lit up with new spotlights, casting huge, distorted shadows across the stone as people pass the sparkling Christmas tree and head up the steps. We follow them through the corridor and down toward the lake, following the crowd and the slightly alarming smell of burning. Venables's idea to light the way to the auditorium with tiny lanterns on boats floating across the lake seems to have been given to Jules Harper, resident pyro. Dad Man gives us a quick wave as he sprints past, fire extinguisher in hand.

The Mothership hurries over to mumble reassuring things to the gathered parental types in posh frocks, shooing them into the foyer. I follow their lead, as if I'm just part of the audience.

The whole place looks adorable. I peep through the auditorium doors to see the silver panels marking off the wings on either side (lined with familiar giant martini glasses) and the glittery ORSINO'S! sign suspended before the plush velvet curtains. A mirror ball revolves above the stage, sending faint hoops of light across the tiered seats, already filling up. But the foyer is decked out in a sparkly new party outfit, too. The walls are draped with balloons and crepe paper streamers. A machine pumps bubbles at the arriving audience, in strange irregular spurts, totally out of time with Huey Lewis thumping out of the crackly speaker system. It looks like a five-year-old's birthday party, only big.

Music Room 1 is the real transformation, though. There's already a crowd of people gathered beneath a glittery sign reading THE VERY LITTLE LEAF, hung over the open doors. As they step aside, they reveal exactly that: the Little Leaf in miniature, like a doll's house version for real people, tucked in beside the usual shelves of glockenspiels and tom-toms. There's the same funny mix of mismatched cups and mugs, tables and chairs. Even the Sofa of Sex has been dragged up the hill for the occasion and plonked in the foyer. I can just see Betsy, pouring out tea, a pair of sparkly stars bouncing off springs on her hairband.

There's a chalkboard behind her, listing the menu: Rubik's Battenburg (for real!), Pop Rock Cakes, Electric Dreams, and all the rest. I'm just being impressed by the highbrow Daily Wisdom — BECAUSE THOU ART VIRTUOUS, THERE SHALL BE NO MORE CAKES (TWELFTH NIGHT, II.iii) APART FROM THESE ONES! — when I get tackled by a French maid and a fifty-foot rollerboy.

"HEIDI!"

I'm on the foyer carpet, with fishnets and skates and hair-spray all over me. Ludo and Dai, who are apparently pleased to see me, to the point of flattening.

"Nice to see you, too?" I say, crawling back to my feet by tugging on Dai's kneepad.

He does an awkward little spin around me on his roller skates, then grabs me again, either in a hug or just to stop himself from rolling into Oliver Bass's mother.

No, it's a hug. Ludo joins in.

"Oh my God, Heidi, we worked it out!"

I detach myself from her arms, and try to guide us out of the path of incoming parents.

"You did?"

She nods wildly, though her backcombed mop of hair stays scarily still.

"We know who he is!" says Dai.

"We're, like, SO stupid!"

"Ridiculous, really. It's been staring us in the face."

"I mean, duh? E?"

I can't even get words out: I just stand there, waiting for them to spill.

"E, Ryder? E for Etienne Gracey?"

They both dance me around, making squeaky noises.

"Etienne Gracey! Isn't it, like, COMPLETELY amazing?"

I nod my head, feeling numb all over.

E.

E for Etienne.

Etienne, who broke up with Scheherezade at the Flick Henshall party.

Etienne, who's going to be wearing a gray leotard with neon pink squiggly bits on it.

I imagine you'll find me easy enough to notice.

It's true. It really is him. Etienne Gracey, Upper School rock god: so cool he even has a band named after him. He really is him.

"Oh my God, Heidi! Like, SMILE?"

"Yeah, Ryder, seriously. It's Etienne Gracey, baby! How awesome is that?"

The crackling of Huey Lewis comes to a sudden stop, and Venables's voice mutters something incomprehensible through the static.

"Oh my God, we're totally supposed to be backstage!"

"Gotta fly. Don't tell me to break a leg or I'll have to kill you!" He skids off into the wall till Ludo grabs him and starts to wheel him toward Music Room 3 and the backstage steps, both cackling gleefully as they wave and wish me luck.

Etienne Gracey.

I still feel numb. That's probably normal, though. That's probably very romantic. I mean, I'm just surprised. It's just ... not what I expected. I'm not disappointed, or anything like that. He's Etienne Gracey, after all. I mean, I've always thought he was a bit self-obsessed and kind of jerky, but E's not like that. And he plays guitar. Ed played guitar. I must like that kind of thing. Maybe that's where I got the idea. That's where this whole thing started, after all: me, sitting on the sofa at the McCartney Party, thinking Etienne liked me. It's come full circle. It all fits together, perfectly, like on the TV.

It just doesn't quite feel like I thought it would, that's all.

I follow the last few people into the auditorium, hesitating in the doorway. The lights go dim, as the last few stragglers take their seats. I can just make out the Mothership waving at me, where she's saved me a place down near the front.

But then the stage lights go up, and there's Henry in pink leggings and a massive pink afro wig, yelling "If music be the food of love, then we're going to need some decibels, baby!" The stage is flooded with flashing lights and smoke. Finches appear: Fili the painted clown on a swing, Dai swirling around on his roller skates, trying not to crush Ludo, as the speakers crackle out "Walk Like an Egyptian." The cloth backdrop falls to reveal Etienne and the Illyrians, in their skintight neon-painted *Tron* bodysuits, miming with huge inflatable instruments.

I don't really want to be here, suddenly. I've been looking forward to this so much, and now I'm here, watching a musical about crazy space disco love, knowing someone who more-than-likes me is up on that stage, and it doesn't feel anything like I'd imagined.

I've messed up again.

I've got what I wanted, and now I don't want it at all.

Yuliya's onstage, towering over Henry in her own fluffy wig, and stumbling her way through her lines slightly inaudibly. Scheherezade and Jambo arrive in a cloud of dry ice, military brass buttons shining, ribbons fluttering in the artificial breeze, to the strains of "Planet Earth." Scheh reappears as a boy, white stripe across her nose, to be flirted with by Henry (all watched by an increasingly intrigued Malcolm Malvolio, aka Dai, to the in-jokey glee of the audience). Fili continues to swing on her trapeze above them all, offering melancholy little snippets of David Bowie between scenes. Etienne and the Illyrians continue to rock out, as far as is possible when your guitars are inflatable and you're surrounded by people dressed as ice-cream cones and cocktail glasses, spinning around to "Club Tropicana."

It's no good. I can't pretend to suddenly like Etienne Gracey, even if he is Mysterious E. I'll have to turn him down, just like Ludo thought I did before, because from now on I'm going to stick to gingerbread boys.

I fumble my way in the dark to the door handle, not daring to watch anymore. I'm going to go and hide away in the Little Leaf for the last time. Drink tea. Eat cake. Maybe a gingerbread man (of the nondusty variety), if they have any.

The auditorium door closes behind me with a whump, blocking out some of the noise, though the speakers still play a static, toned-down version, and there's a small TV screen showing the view from the very edge of the stage, courtesy of Venables's camera. It's cooler out here, at least. I creep over to the makeshift counter beneath the glittery sign, and find not Betsy but Teddy, propped on his elbows. He gives me one of his lazy smiles, then goes back to watching the show on the TV, chuckling at Ludo and Dai falling about.

"Your costumes look awesome," I say, over the music.

Teddy shakes his head. "Team effort, please. They were your ideas, remember?"

I shrug back. I've made sure his name's in the program, but I still feel guilty. It's kind of cheeky of me to ask him for anything more — but this one's not for me. I might be incapable of sorting out my own love life, but at least I can add a quick fizz to someone else's.

"Can I ask a little favor? It's kind of mental. And I did sort of ask you before, and you said no, and you can totally say no again, if you think it's a horrible idea, only it would totally make her night, and I kind of feel like I owe her that, so . . ."

Teddy looks amused at me stumbling over my words, and twirls his finger, to speed me up.

"I just wondered if you wouldn't mind kissing Ludo." It sounds very mental, now I've said it: Now his eyebrows have shot up into his hair. "I mean, only the once. And not a huge full-on snogathon. Unless you wanted to."

"Heidi," says Teddy, gently, almost apologetic. "I don't want to kiss Ludo."

"Right. Sorry. You could just give her a hug, even? No, forget I said that. Forget I said anything? Just erase all memory of this conversation?"

The easy smile spreads across his face again. I shuffle my feet: Guess I deserve being laughed at. Should be used it from Teddy anyway. I wait for him to make some snarky comment about how I'm very easily forgettable, or whatever, but he's looking up. Not at the TV, or at the ceiling: looking up and tipping his head back a little, as if he wants me to look up above his head.

The Shakespearean Daily Wisdom has been wiped away. In its place, in Teddy's familiar twirly handwriting, it says:

MUST I SPELL IT OUT?! *YOU HAVE MY LOVE & AFFECTION, TEDDY.*

OH.

MY.

GOD.

My hand flies to my mouth. I think some kind of squeaky noise gets out anyway.

"It's really that much of a surprise?" he says, his face falling.

I squeak again.

Yes?

"Yes, it is, it is, but . . . yes!"

He scrunches up one eye. "Could you say that again, because only dogs can hear you right now, and I'm sort of invested in the answer?"

I drop my hand away, and I wrap my other around it to stop it shaking. Rest them both on the counter. Let one creep forward, and take hold of one of his.

"Yes," I say, still all breathy and mouselike. "But . . . good surprise?"

That smile comes along again. That Teddy smile that I've

watched from afar: that I never, ever imagined could be for me.

"But . . . but . . . how? And when did you . . . ? And . . . why did you . . . ?"

"I've always thought you were pretty awesome, you know, on account of you actually being pretty awesome. Then suddenly you were inventing this boyfriend for yourself, and I thought, hey, wait up, I'm feeling kind of jealous of this guy. Well, I think Safak was the one who figured that out, actually. She thought it was kind of interesting you'd called him Ed. You know: Eddie . . . Teddy?"

I decide not to explain about E. D. Hartley: It can probably be saved for later.

"We didn't really break up because of *Tron*, either," he adds, looking faintly embarrassed.

"What? But — I didn't mean you to do that! I mean, she was really lovely!"

"Yeah. But, so are you. She noticed I thought so anyway. Mostly from me renting a movie I knew you'd love. Maybe we did break up because of *Tron* after all. . . ."

"But why didn't you say anything?"

"Says the girl with the gingerbread boyfriend? I don't know, I thought the whole 'E' thing would be cute. Mom kept watching those DVDs of that show you like, and . . . well, guess I was trying to cover my ass a little, too. That Ed guy was kind of intimidating to live up to, you know?'

His hand tightens around mine, just slightly. Teddy's

hand. Teddy's hand, holding my hand, as if it doesn't want to let go.

"And I figured I was being pretty obvious — till you thought E was basically any unavailable, inappropriate guy in a forty-mile radius who wasn't me."

I bite my lip, feeling guilty again, though he's smiling.

There's a burst of static from the speakers. I glance over at the TV screen, and catch Etienne Gracey in his leotard, thwacking Brendan around the head with his deflating guitar. I decide not to mention him, either. Though I don't think anything could ruin this moment: me, and him, my E, my perfect, not-imaginary, better-than-imaginary boy.

"Oh! But . . . you're going away!"

He sighs, dropping his head.

"Not for another week. And we'll be back to visit? But yeah, I know. I figured we'd work this out a little quicker. But you're kind of a master at e-mail relationships already, right? If you think about it, we've been going out for weeks already, without even meeting. You think an ocean's going to get in our way?"

I shake my head, biting my lip to keep the squeakiness inside.

"Now, dearest Heidi, I have but one question to ask," he says, adopting a slightly wonky accent and attempting to look very serious, despite the on-screen vision of Honey Prentiss skipping across the stage dressed as a giant pink shoe. "And quit laughing, I worked pretty hard at learning how to talk like some stiff-assed Brit guy. So, dearest Heidi, my question?"

"Yes, Rupert?"

He gives me a stern look, then leans closer, a wicked twinkle in his eye.

"Still want me to kiss Ludo?" he whispers.

The speakers blare out "Take on Me," improbably on cue.

I shake my head.

I lean closer.

He doesn't taste like gingerbread.

Although I should probably kiss him again, just to make sure.

Recipe for Love

INGREDIENTS:

Heidi
Teddy

METHOD:

• Just leave them to it.

○ ○

A dimly lit penthouse. Mycroft Christie, heroic detective, peers out of the wardrobe, looking slightly peeved to see every available surface in the apartment now covered with small, delicious-smelling gingerbread men. Glamorous Miss Heidi Ryder is a bit busy reading her e-mails to notice.

to: arealboy@letterbox.com
from: heidi.ryder@goldfinch.ac.uk

Dearest T,

Have you added more cinnamon? Extra yummy this week

anyway. Though the postman is starting to think I'm involved in a thrilling international import/export crime syndicate.

I & a,

H

to: heidi.ryder@goldfinch.ac.uk
from: arealboy@letterbox.com

Dearest Heidi,

Same here. Mom says, "Thanks for the teabags, now send another five million or so."

They weren't yummy before? I'm sulking here.

I & a,

T

to: arealboy@letterbox.com
from: heidi.ryder@goldfinch.ac.uk

Dearest T,

I'm sure the postman will just love me for that. Tell her she'll just have to visit?

Yumminess never in doubt, I promise. :)

l & a,

H

Dearest Heidi,

I don't know that they'd let her through customs, with that weird guy-shaped lump in her suitcase. Anyway, I hear the girl she might really want to visit spends all her time on the internet, talking to some boy.

At least that's what she says. He sounds improbable to me.

l & a,

T

Dearest T,

Improbable boys are nice. But I like real ones best of all.

l & a,

H

The End